The
Celebrity

Winston Churchill

1ˢᵗ WORLD
LIBRARY
Literary Society

The Celebrity

Winston Churchill

© 1st World Library – Literary Society, 2004
PO Box 2211
Fairfield, IA 52556
www.1stworldlibrary.org
First Edition

LCCN: 2003099811

ISBN: 1-59540-134-2

Purchase *"The Celebrity"*
as a traditional bound book at:
www.1stWorldLibrary.org/purchase.asp?ISBN=1-59540-134-2

1st World Library Literary Society is a nonprofit
organization dedicated to promoting literacy by:

- Creating a free internet library accessible from any
  computer worldwide.
- Hosting writing competitions and offering book
  publishing scholarships.

Readers interested in supporting literacy
through sponsorship, donations or
membership please contact:
literacy@1stworldlibrary.org
Check us out at: www.1stworldlibrary.org

The Celebrity
contributed by Ed, Tim & Rodney
in support of
1st World Library Literary Society

VOLUME 1.

CHAPTER I

I was about to say that I had known the Celebrity from the time he wore kilts. But I see I shall have to amend that, because he was not a celebrity then, nor, indeed, did he achieve fame until some time after I had left New York for the West. In the old days, to my commonplace and unobserving mind, he gave no evidences of genius whatsoever. He never read me any of his manuscripts, which I can safely say he would have done had he written any at that time, and therefore my lack of detection of his promise may in some degree be pardoned. But he had then none of the oddities and mannerisms which I hold to be inseparable from genius, and which struck my attention in after days when I came in contact with the Celebrity. Hence I am constrained to the belief that his eccentricity must have arrived with his genius, and both after the age of twenty-five. Far be it from me to question the talents of one upon whose head has been set the laurel of fame!

When I knew him he was a young man without frills or foibles, with an excellent head for business. He was starting in to practise law in a downtown office with the intention of becoming a great corporation lawyer. He used to drop into my chambers once in a while to smoke, and was first-rate company. When I gave a dinner there was generally a cover laid for him. I liked the man for his own sake, and even had he promised to turn out a celebrity it would have had no weight with me. I look upon notoriety with the same indifference as on the buttons on a man's shirt-front, or the crest on his note-paper.

When I went West, he fell out of my life. I probably should not have given him another thought had I not caught sight of his name, in old capitals, on a daintily covered volume in a book-stand. I had little time or inclination for reading fiction; my days were busy ones, and my nights were spent with law books. But I bought the volume out of curiosity, wondering the while whether he could have written it. I was soon set at rest, for the dedication was to a young woman of whom I had often heard him speak. The volume was a collection of short stories. On these I did not feel myself competent to sit in judgment, for my personal taste in fiction, if I could be said to have had any, took another turn. The stories dealt mainly with the affairs of aristocratic young men and aristocratic young women, and were differentiated to fit situations only met with in that society which does not have to send descriptions of its functions to the newspapers. The stories did not seem to me to touch life. They were plainly intended to have a bracing moral effect, and perhaps had this result for the people at whom they were aimed. They left with me the impression of a well-delivered stereopticon lecture, with characters about as life-like as the shadows on the screen, and whisking on and off, at the mercy of the operator. Their charm to me lay in the manner of the telling, the style, which I am forced to admit was delightful.

But the book I had bought was a success, a great success, if the newspapers and the reports of the sales were to be trusted. I read the criticisms out of curiosity more than any other prompting, and no two of them were alike: they veered from extreme negative to extreme positive. I have to confess that it gratified me not a little to find the negatives for the most part of my poor way of thinking. The positives, on the other hand, declared the gifted young author to have found a manner of treatment of social life entirely new. Other critics still insisted it was social ridicule: but if this were so, the satire was too delicate for ordinary detection.

However, with the dainty volume my quondam friend sprang into fame. At the same time he cast off the chrysalis of a commonplace existence. He at once became the hero of the young women of the country from Portland, Maine, to Portland, Oregon, many of whom wrote him letters and asked him for his photograph. He was asked to tell what he really meant by the vague endings of this or that story. And then I began to hear rumors that his head was turning. These I discredited, of course. If true, I thought it but another proof of the undermining influence of feminine flattery, which few men, and fewer young men, can stand. But I watched his career with interest.

He published other books, of a high moral tone and unapproachable principle, which I read carefully for some ray of human weakness, for some stroke of nature untrammelled by the calling code of polite society. But in vain.

CHAPTER II

It was by a mere accident that I went West, some years ago, and settled in an active and thriving town near one of the Great Lakes. The air and bustle and smack of life about the place attracted me, and I rented an office and continued to read law, from force of habit, I suppose. My experience in the service of one of the most prominent of New York lawyers stood me in good stead, and gradually, in addition to a heterogeneous business of mines and lumber, I began to pick up a few clients. But in all probability I should be still pegging away at mines and lumber, and drawing up occasional leases and contracts, had it not been for Mr. Farquhar Fenelon Cooke, of Philadelphia. Although it has been specifically written that promotion to a young man comes neither from the East nor the West, nor yet from the South, Mr. Cooke arrived from the East, and in the nick of time for me.

I was indebted to Farrar for Mr. Cooke's acquaintance, and this obligation I have since in vain endeavored to repay. Farrar's profession was forestry: a graduate of an eastern college, he had gone abroad to study, and had roughed it with the skilled woodsmen of the Black Forest. Mr. Cooke, whom he represented, had large tracts of land in these parts, and Farrar likewise received an income from the state, whose legislature had at last opened its eyes to the timber depredations and had begun to buy up reserves. We had rooms in the same Elizabethan building at the corner of Main and Superior streets, but it was more than a year before I got farther than a nod with him. Farrar's nod in itself was a repulsion, and once you had seen it you mentally scored him from the list of your possible friends. Besides this freezing exterior he possessed a cutting and cynical tongue, and had but little confidence in the human race. These qualities did not tend to render him popular in a Western town, if indeed they would have recommended him anywhere, and I confess to have thought him a surly enough fellow, being guided by general opinion and superficial observation. Afterwards the town got to know him, and if it did not precisely like him, it respected him, which perhaps is better. And he gained at least a few warm-friends, among whom I deem it an honor to be mentioned.

Farrar's contempt for consequences finally brought him an unsought-for reputation. Admiration for him was born the day he pushed O'Meara out of his office and down a flight of stairs because he had undertaken to suggest that which should be done with the timber in Jackson County. By this summary proceeding Farrar lost the support of a faction, O'Meara being a power in the state and chairman of the forestry board besides. But he got rid of interference from that day forth.

Oddly enough my friendship with Farrar was an indirect result of the incident I have just related. A few mornings after, I was seated in my office trying to concentrate my mind on page twenty of volume ten of the Records when I was surprised by O'Meara himself, accompanied by two gentlemen whom I remembered to have seen on various witness stands. O'Meara was handsomely dressed, and his necktie made but a faint pretence of concealing the gorgeous diamond in his shirt-front. But his face wore an aggrieved air, and his left hand was neatly bound in black and tucked into his coat. He sank comfortably into my wicker chair, which creaked a protest, and produced two yellow-spotted cigars, chewing the end of one with much apparent relish and pushing the other at me. His two friends remained respectfully standing. I guessed at what was coming, and braced myself by refusing the cigar, - not a great piece of self-denial, by the way. But a case meant much to me then, and I did seriously regret that O'Meara was not a possible client. At any rate, my sympathy with Farrar in the late episode put him out of the question.

O'Meara cleared his throat and began gingerly to undo the handkerchief on his hand. Then he brought his fist down on the table so that the ink started from the stand and his cheeks shook with the effort.

"I'll make him pay for this!" he shouted, with an oath,

The other gentlemen nodded their approval, while I put the inkstand in a place of safety.

"You're a pretty bright young man, Mr. Crocker," he went on, a look of cunning coming into his little eyes, "but I guess you ain't had too many cases to object to a big one."

"Did you come here to tell me that?" I asked.

He looked me over queerly, and evidently decided that I meant no effrontery.

"I came here to get your opinion," he said, holding up a

swollen hand, "but I want to tell you first that I ought to get ten thousand, not a cent less. That scoundrelly young upstart - "

"If you want my opinion," I replied, trying to speak slowly, "it is that Mr. Farrar ought to get ten thousand dollars. And I think that would be only a moderate reward."

I did not feel equal to pushing him into the street, as Farrar had done, and I have now but a vague notion of what he said and how he got there. But I remember that half an hour afterwards a man congratulated me openly in the bank.

That night I found a new friend, although at the time I thought Farrar's visit to me the accomplishment of a perfunctory courtesy to a man who had refused to take a case against him. It was very characteristic of Farrar not to mention this until he rose to go. About half-past eight he sauntered in upon me, placing his hat precisely on the rack, and we talked until ten, which is to say that I talked and he commented. His observations were apt, if a trifle caustic, and it is needless to add that I found them entertaining. As he was leaving he held out his hand.

"I hear that O'Meara called on you to-day," he said diffidently.

"Yes," I answered, smiling, "I was sorry not to have been able to take his case."

I sat up for an hour or more, trying to arrive at some conclusion about Farrar, but at length I gave it up. His visit had in it something impulsive which I could not reconcile with his manner. He surely owed me nothing for refusing a case against him, and must have known that my motives for so doing were not personal. But if I did not understand him, I liked him decidedly from that night forward, and I hoped that his advances had sprung from some other motive than politeness. And indeed we gradually drifted into a quasi-friendship. It became his habit, as he went out in the morning, to drop into my room for a match, and I returned the compliment by borrowing his coal oil when mine was out. At such times we would sit, or more frequently stand, discussing the affairs of the town and of the nation, for politics was an easy and attractive subject to us both. It was only in a general way that we touched upon each other's concerns, this being dangerous ground with Farrar, who was ever ready to close up at anything resembling a confidence. As for me, I hope I am not curious, but I own to having had a curiosity about Farrar's Philadelphia patron, to whom Farrar made but slight allusions. His very name - Farquhar Fenelon Cooke - had an odd sound which somehow betokened an odd man, and there was more than one bit of gossip afloat in the town of which he was the subject, notwithstanding the fact that he had never honored it with a visit. The gossip was the natural result of Mr. Cooke's large properties in the vicinity. It has never been my habit, however, to press a friend on such matters, and I could easily understand and respect Farrar's reluctance to talk of one from whom he received an income.

I had occasion, in the May of that year, to make a somewhat long business trip to Chicago, and on my return, much to my surprise, I found Farrar awaiting me in the railroad station. He smiled his wonted fraction by way of greeting, stopped to buy a newspaper, and finally leading me to his buggy, turned and drove out of town. I was completely mystified at such an unusual proceeding.

"What's this for?" I asked.

"I shan't bother you long," he said; "I simply wanted the chance to talk to you before you got to your office. I have a Philadelphia client, a Mr. Cooke, of whom you may have heard me speak. Since you have been away the railroad has brought suit against him. The row is about the lands west of the Washita, on Copper Rise. It's the devil if he loses, for the ground is worth the dollar bills to cover it. I telegraphed, and he got here yesterday. He wants a lawyer, and I mentioned you."

There came over me then in a flash a comprehension of Farrar which I had failed to grasp before. But I was quite overcome at his suggestion.

"Isn't it rather a big deal to risk me on?" I said. "Better go to Chicago and get Parks. He's an expert in that sort of thing." I am afraid my expostulation was weak.

"I merely spoke of you," replied Farrar, coolly, - and he has gone around to your office. He knows about Parks, and if he wants him he'll probably take him. It all depends upon how you strike Cooke whether you get the case or not. I have never told you about him," he added with some hesitation; "he's a trifle queer, but a good fellow at the bottom. I should hate to see him lose his land."

"How is the railroad mixed up in it?" I asked.

"I don't know much about law, but it would seem as if they had a pretty strong case," he answered. He went on to tell me what he knew of the matter in his clean, pithy sentences, often brutally cynical, as though he had not a spark of interest in any of it. Mr. Cooke's claim to the land came from a maternal great-uncle, long since deceased, who had been a settler in these regions. The railroad answered that they had bought the land with other properties from the man, also deceased, to whom the old gentleman was alleged to have sold it. Incidentally I learned something of Mr. Cooke's maternal ancestry.

We drove back to the office with some concern on my part at the prospect of so large a case. Sunning himself on the board steps, I saw for the first time Mr. Farquhar Fenelon Cooke. He was dressed out in broad gaiters and bright tweeds, like an English tourist, and his face might have belonged to Dagon, idol of the Philistines. A silver snaffle on a heavy leather watch guard which connected the pockets of his corduroy waistcoat, together with a huge gold stirrup in his Ascot tie, sufficiently proclaimed his tastes. But I found myself continually returning to the countenance, and I still think I could have modelled a better face out of putty. The mouth was rather small, thick-tipped, and put in at an odd angle; the brown eyes were large, and from their habit of looking up at one lent to the round face an incongruous solemnity. But withal there was a perceptible acumen about the man which was puzzling in the extreme.

"How are you, old man?" said he, hardly waiting for Farrar to introduce me. "Well, I hope." It was pure cordiality, nothing more. He seemed to bubble over with it.

I said I was well, and invited him inside.

"No," he said; "I like the look of the town. We can talk business here."

And talk business he did, straight and to the point, so fast and indistinctly that at times I could scarcely follow him. I answered his rapid questions briefly, and as best I knew how. He wanted to know what chance he had to win the suit, and I told him there might be other factors involved beside those of which he had spoken. Plainly, also, that the character of his great-uncle was in question, an intimation which he did not appear to resent. But that there was no denying the fact that the railroad had a strong thing of it, and a good lawyer into the bargain.

"And don't you consider yourself a good lawyer?" he cut in.

I pointed out that the railroad lawyer was a man of twice my age, experience, and reputation.

Without more ado, and before either Farrar or myself had time to resist, he had hooked an arm into each of us, and we were all three marching down the street in the direction of his hotel. If this was agony for me, I could see that it was keener agony for Farrar. And although Mr. Farquhar Fenelon Cooke had been in town but a scant twenty-four hours, it seemed as if he knew more of its inhabitants than both of us put together. Certain it is that he was less particular with his acquaintances. He hailed the most astonishing people with an easy air of freedom, now releasing my arm, now Farrar's, to salute. He always saluted. He stopped to converse with a dozen men we had never seen, many of whom smelled strongly of the stable, and he invariably introduced Farrar as the forester of his estate, and me as his lawyer in the great quarrel with the railroad, until I began to wish I had never heard of Blackstone. And finally he steered us into the spacious bar of the Lake House.

The next morning the three of us were off early for a look at the contested property. It was a twenty-mile drive, and the last eight miles wound down the boiling Washita, still high with the melting snows of the pine lands. And even here the snows yet slept in the deeper hollows. unconscious of the budding green of the slopes. How heartily I wished Mr. Farquhar Fenelon Cooke back in Philadelphia! By his eternal accounts of his Germantown stables and of the blue ribbons of his hackneys he killed all sense of pleasure of the scene, and set up an irritation that was well-nigh unbearable. At length we crossed the river, climbed the foot-hills, and paused on the ridge. Below us lay the quaint inn and scattered cottages of Asquith, and beyond them the limitless and foam-flecked expanse of lake: and on our right, lifting from the shore by easy slopes for a mile at stretch, Farrar pointed out the timbered lands of Copper Rise, spread before us like a map. But the appreciation of beauty formed no part of Mr. Cooke's composition, - that is, beauty as Farrar and I knew it.

"If you win that case, old man," he cried, striking me a great whack between the shoulderblades," charge any fee you like; I'll pay it! And I'll make such a country-place out of this as was never seen west of New York state, and call it Mohair, after my old trotter. I'll put a palace on that clearing, with the stables just over the knoll. They'll beat the Germantown stables a whole lap. And that strip of level," he continued, pointing to a thinly timbered bit, "will hold a mile track nicely."

Farrar and I gasped: it was as if we had tumbled into the Washita.

"It will take money, Mr. Cooke," said Farrar, "and you haven't won the suit yet."

"Damn the money!" said Mr. Cooke, and we knew he meant it.

Over the episodes of that interminable morning it will, be better to pass lightly. It was spent by Farrar and me in misery. It was spent by Mr. Farquhar Fenelon Cooke in an ecstasy of enjoyment, driving over and laying out Mohair, and I must admit he evinced a surprising genius in his planning, although, according to Farrar, he broke every sacred precept of landscape gardening again and again. He displayed the enthusiasm of a pioneer, and the energy of a Napoleon. And if he were too ignorant to accord to nature a word of praise, he had the grace and intelligence to compliment Farrar on the superb condition of the forests, and on the judgment shown in laying out the roads, which were so well chosen that even in this season they were well drained and dry. That day, too, my views were materially broadened, and I received an insight into the methods and possibilities of my friend's profession sufficient to instil a deeper respect both for it and for him. The crowded spots had been skilfully thinned of the older trees to give the younger ones a chance, and the harmony of the whole had been carefully worked out. Now we drove under dark pines and hemlocks, and then into a lighter relief of birches and wild cherries, or a copse of young beeches. And I learned that the estate had not only been paying the taxes and its portion of Farrar's salary, but also a considerable amount into Mr. Cooke's pocket the while it was being improved.

Mr. Cooke made his permanent quarters at the Lake House, and soon became one of the best-known characters about town. He seemed to enjoy his popularity, and I am convinced that he would have been popular in spite of his now-famous quarrel with the railroad. His easy command of profanity, his generous use of money, his predilection for sporting characters, of whom he was king; his ready geniality and good-fellowship alike with the clerk of the Lake House or the Mayor, not to mention his own undeniable personality, all combined to make him a favorite. He had his own especial table in the dining-room, called all the waiters by their first names, and they fought for the privilege of attending him. He likewise called the barkeepers by their first names, and had his own particular corner of the bar, where none dared intrude, and where he could almost invariably be found when not in my office. From this corner he dealt out cigars to the deserving, held stake moneys, decided all bets, and refereed all differences. His name appeared in the personal column of one of the local papers on the average of twice a week, or in lieu thereof one of his choicest stories in the "Notes about Town" column.

The case was to come up early in July, and I spent most of my time, to the detriment of other affairs, in preparing for it. I was greatly hampered in my work by my client, who filled my office with his tobacco-smoke and that of his friends, and he took it very much for granted that he was going to win the suit. Fortune had always played into his hands, he said, and I had no little difficulty in convincing him that matters had passed from his hands into mine. In this I believe I was never entirely successful. I soon found, too, that he had no ideas whatever on the value of discretion, and it was only by repeated threats of absolute failure that I prevented our secret tactics from becoming the property of his sporting fraternity and of the town.

The more I worked on the case, the clearer it became to me that Mr. Farquhar Fenelon Cooke's great-uncle had been either a consummate scoundrel or a lunatic, and that our only hope of winning must be based on proving him one or the other; it did not matter much which, for my expectations at best were small. When I had at length settled to this conclusion I confided it as delicately as possible to my client, who was sitting at the time with his feet cocked up on the office table, reading a pink newspaper.

"Which'll be the easier to prove?" he asked, without looking up.

"It would be more charitable to prove he had been out of his mind," I replied, "and perhaps easier."

"Charity be damned," said this remarkable man. "I'm after the property."

So I decided on insanity. I hunted up and subpoenaed white-haired witnesses for miles around. Many of them shook their heads when they spoke of Mr. Cooke's great-uncle, and some knew more of his private transactions than I could have wished, and I trembled lest my own witnesses should be turned against me. I learned more of Mr. Cooke's great-uncle than I knew of Mr. Cooke himself, and to the credit of my client be it said that none of his relative's traits were apparent in him, with the possible exception of insanity; and that defect, if it existed in the grand-nephew, took in him a milder and less criminal turn. The old rascal, indeed, had so cleverly worded his deed of sale as to obtain payment without transfer. It was a trifle easier to avoid being specific in that country in his day than it is now, and the document was, in my opinion, sufficiently vague to admit of a double meaning. The original sale had been made to a man, now dead, whom the railroad had bought out. The Copper Rise property was mentioned among the other lands in the will in favor of Mr. Farquhar Fenelon Cooke, and the latter had gone ahead improving them and increasing their output in spite of the repeated threats of the railroad to bring suit. And it was not until its present attorney had come in and investigated the title that the railroad had resorted to the law. I mention here, by the way, that my client was the sole heir.

But as the time of the sessions drew near, the outlook for me was anything but bright. It is true that my witnesses were quite willing to depose that his actions were queer and out of the common, but these witnesses were for the most part venerable farmers and backwoodsmen: expert testimony was deplorably lacking. In this extremity it was Mr. Farquhar Fenelon Cooke himself who came unwittingly to my rescue. He had bought a horse, - he could never be in a place long without one, - which was chiefly remarkable, he said, for picking up his hind feet as well as his front ones. However he may have differed from the ordinary run of horses, he was shortly attacked by one of the thousand ills to which every horse is subject. I will not pretend to say what it was. I found Mr. Cooke one morning at his usual place in the Lake House bar holding forth with more than common vehemence and profanity on the subject of veterinary surgeons. He declared there was not a veterinary surgeon in the whole town fit to hold a certificate, and his listeners nodded an extreme approval to this sentiment. A grizzled old fellow who kept a stock farm back in the country chanced to be there, and managed to get a word in on the subject during one of my client's rare pauses.

"Yes," he said, "that's so. There ain't one of 'em now fit to travel with young Doctor Vane, who was here some fifteen years gone by. He weren't no horse-doctor, but he could fix up a foundered horse in a night as good as new. If your uncle was livin', he'd back me on that, Mr. Cooke."

Here was my chance. I took the old man aside, and two or three glasses of Old Crow launched him into reminiscence.

"Where is Doctor Vane now?" I asked finally.

"Over to Minneapolis, sir, with more rich patients nor he can take care of. Wasn't my darter over there last month, and seen him? And demned if he didn't pull up his carriage and talk to her. Here's luck to him."

I might have heard much more of the stockraiser had I stayed, but I fear I left him somewhat abruptly in my haste to find Farrar. Only three days remained before the case was to come up. Farrar readily agreed to go to Minneapolis, and was off on the first train that afternoon. I would have asked Mr. Cooke to go had I dared trust him, such was my anxiety to have him out of the way, if only for a time. I did not tell him about the doctor. He sat up very late with me that night on the Lake House porch to give me a rubbing down, as he expressed it, as he might have admonished some favorite jockey before a sweepstake. "Take it easy, old man," he would say repeatedly, "and don't give things the bit before you're sure of their wind!"

Days passed, and not a word from Farrar. The case opened with Mr. Cooke's friends on the front benches. The excitement it caused has rarely been equalled in that section, but I believe this was due less to its sensational features than to Mr. Cooke, who had an abnormal though unconscious talent for self-advertisement. It became manifest early that we were losing. Our testimony, as I had feared, was not strong enough, although they said we were making a good fight of it. I was racked with anxiety about Farrar; at last, when I had all but given up hope, I received a telegram from him dated at Detroit, saying he would arrive with the doctor that evening. This was Friday, the fourth day of the trial.

The doctor turned out to be a large man, well groomed and well fed, with a twinkle in his eye. He had gone to Narragansett Pier for the summer, whither Farrar had followed him. On being introduced, Mr. Cooke at once invited him out to have a drink.

"Did you know my uncle?" asked my client.

"Yes," said the doctor," I should say I did."

"Poor old duffer," said Mr. Cooke, with due solemnity; "I understand he was a maniac."

"Well," said the doctor, while we listened with a

breathless interest, "he wasn't exactly a maniac, but I think I can safely say he was a lunatic."

"Then here's to insanity!" said the irrepressible, his glass swung in mid-air, when a thought struck him, and he put it down again and looked hard at the doctor.

"Will you swear to it?" he demanded.

"I would swear to it before Saint Peter," said the doctor, fervently.

He swore to it before a jury, which was more to the point, and we won our case. It did not even go to the court of appeals; I suppose the railroad thought it cheaper to drop it, since no right of way was involved. And the decision was scarcely announced before Mr. Farquhar Fenelon Cooke had begun work on his new country place, Mohair.

I have oftentimes been led to consider the relevancy of this chapter, and have finally decided to insert it. I concluded that the actual narrative of how Mr. Cooke came to establish his country-place near Asquith would be interesting, and likewise throw some light on that gentleman's character. And I ask the reader's forbearance for the necessary personal history involved. Had it not been for Mr. Cooke's friendship for me I should not have written these pages.

CHAPTER III

Events, are consequential or inconsequential irrespective of their size. The wars of Troy were fought for a woman, and Charles VIII, of France, bumped his head against a stone doorway and died because he did not stoop low enough. And to descend from history down to my own poor chronicle, Mr. Cooke's railroad case, my first experience at the bar of any gravity or magnitude, had tied to it a string of consequences then far beyond my guessing. The suit was my stepping-stone not only to a larger and more remunerative practice, but also, I believe, to the position of district attorney, which I attained shortly afterwards.

Mr. Cooke had laid out Mohair as ruthlessly as Napoleon planned the new Paris; though not, I regret to say, with a like genius. Fortunately Farrar interposed and saved the grounds, but there was no guardian angel to do a like turn for the house. Mr. Langdon Willis, of Philadelphia, was the architect who had nominal charge of the building. He had regularly submitted some dozen plans for Mr. Cooke's approval, which were as regularly rejected. My client believed, in common with a great many other people, that architects should be driven and not followed, and was plainly resolved to make this house the logical development of many cherished ideas. It is not strange, therefore, that the edifice was completed by a Chicago contractor who had less self-respect than Mr. Willis, the latter having abruptly refused to have his name tacked on to the work.

Mohair was finished and ready for occupation in July, two years after the suit. I drove out one day before Mr. Cooke's arrival to look it over. The grounds, where Farrar had had matters pretty much his own way, to my mind rivalled the best private parks in the East. The stables were filled with a score or so of Mr. Cooke's best horses, brought hither in his private cars, and the trotters were exercising on the track. The middle of June found Farrar and myself at the Asquith Inn. It was Farrar's custom to go to Asquith in the summer, being near the forest properties in his charge; and since Asquith was but five miles from the county-seat it was convenient for me, and gave me the advantages of the lake breezes and a comparative rest, which I should not have had in town. At that time Asquith was a small community of summer residents from Cincinnati, Chicago, St. Louis, and other western cities, most of whom owned cottages and the grounds around them. They were a quiet lot that long association had made clannish; and they had a happy faculty, so rare in summer resorts, of discrimination between an amusement and a nuisance. Hence a great many diversions which are accounted pleasurable elsewhere are at Asquith set down at their true value. It was, therefore, rather with resentment than otherwise that the approaching arrival of Mr. Cooke and the guests he was likely to have at Mohair were looked upon.

I had not been long at Asquith before I discovered that Farrar was acting in a peculiar manner, though I was longer in finding out what the matter was. I saw much less of him than in town. Once in a while in the evenings, after ten, he would run across me on the porch of the inn, or drift into my rooms. Even after three years of more or less intimacy between us, Farrar still wore his exterior of pessimism and indifference, the shell with which he chose to hide a naturally warm and affectionate disposition. In the dining-room we sat together at the end of a large table set aside for bachelors and small families of two or three, and it seemed as though we had all the humorists and story-tellers in that place. And Farrar as a source of amusement proved equal to the best of them. He would wait until a story was well under way, and then annihilate the point of it with a cutting cynicism and set the table in a roar of laughter. Among others who were seated here was a Mr. Trevor, of Cincinnati, one of the pioneers of Asquith. Mr. Trevor was a trifle bombastic, with a tendency towards gesticulation, an art which he had learned in no less a school than the Ohio State Senate. He was a self-made man, - a fact which he took good care should not escape one, - and had amassed his money, I believe, in the dry-goods business. He always wore a long, shiny coat, a low, turned-down collar, and a black tie, all of which united to give him the general appearance of a professional pallbearer.

But Mr. Trevor possessed a daughter who amply made up for his shortcomings. She was the only one who could meet Farrar on his own ground, and rarely a meal passed that they did not have a tilt. They filled up the holes of the conversation with running commentaries, giving a dig at the luckless narrator and a side-slap at each other, until one would have given his oath they were sworn enemies. At least I, in the innocence of my heart, thought so until I was forcibly enlightened. I had taken rather a prejudice to Miss

Trevor. I could find no better reason than her antagonism to Farrar. I was revolving this very thing in my mind one day as I was paddling back to the inn after a look at my client's new pier and boat-houses, when I descried Farrar's catboat some distance out. The lake was glass, and the sail hung lifeless. It was near lunch-time, and charity prompted me to head for the boat and give it a tow homeward. As I drew near, Farrar himself emerged from behind the sail and asked me, with a great show of nonchalance, what I wanted.

"To tow you back for lunch, of course," I answered, used to his ways.

He threw me a line, which I made fast to the stern, and then he disappeared again. I thought this somewhat strange, but as the boat was a light one, I towed it in and hitched it to the wharf, when, to my great astonishment, there disembarked not Farrar, but Miss Trevor. She leaped lightly ashore and was gone before I could catch my breath, while Farrar let down the sail and offered me a cigarette. I had learned a lesson in appearances.

It could not have been very long after this that I was looking over my batch of New York papers, which arrived weekly, when my eye was arrested by a name. I read the paragraph, which announced the fact that my friend the Celebrity was about to sail for Europe in search of "color" for his next novel; this was already contracted for at a large price, and was to be of a more serious nature than any of his former work. An interview was published in which the Celebrity had declared that a new novel was to appear in a short time. I do not know what impelled me, but I began at once to search through the other papers, and found almost identically the same notice in all of them.

By one of those odd coincidents which sometimes start one to thinking, the Celebrity was the subject of a lively discussion when I reached the table that evening. I had my quota of information concerning his European trip, but I did not commit myself when appealed to for an opinion. I had once known the man (which, however, I did not think it worth while to mention) and I did not feel justified in criticising him in public. Besides, what I knew of him was excellent, and entirely apart from the literary merit or demerit of his work. The others, however, were within their right when they censured or praised him, and they did both. Farrar, in particular, surprised me by the violence of his attacks, while Miss Trevor took up the Celebrity's defence with equal ardor. Her motives were beyond me now. The Celebrity's works spoke for themselves, she said, and she could not and would not believe such injurious reports of one who wrote as he did.

The next day I went over to the county-seat, and got back to Asquith after dark. I dined alone, and afterwards I was strolling up and down one end of the long veranda when I caught sight of a lonely figure in a corner, with chair tilted back and feet on the rail. A gleam of a cigar lighted up the face, and I saw that it was Farrar. I sat down beside him, and we talked commonplaces for a while, Farrar's being almost monosyllabic, while now and again feminine voices and feminine laughter reached our ears from the far end of the porch. They seemed to go through Farrar like a knife, and he smoked furiously, his lips tightly compressed the while. I had a dozen conjectures, none of which I dared voice. So I waited in patience.

"Crocker," said he, at length, "there's a man here from Boston, Charles Wrexell Allen; came this morning. You know Boston. Have you ever heard of him?"

"Allen," I repeated, reflecting; "no Charles Wrexell."

"It is Charles Wrexell, I think," said Farrar, as though the matter were trivial. "However, we can go into the register and make sure."

"What about him?" I asked, not feeling inclined to stir.

The Celebrity

"Oh, nothing. An arrival is rather an occurrence, though. You can hear him down there now," he added, tossing his head towards the other end of the porch, "with the women around him."

In fact, I did catch the deeper sound of a man's voice among the lighter tones, and the voice had a ring to it which was not wholly unfamiliar, although I could not place it.

I threw Farrar a bait.

"He must make friends easily," I said.

"With the women? - yes," he replied, so scathingly that I was forced to laugh in spite of myself.

"Let us go in and look at the register," I suggested. "You may have his name wrong."

We went in accordingly. Sure enough, in bold, heavy characters, was the name Charles Wrexell Allen written out in full. That handwriting was one in a thousand. I made sure I had seen it before, and yet I did not know it; and the more I puzzled over it the more confused I became. I turned to Farrar.

"I have had a poor cigar passed off on me and deceive me for a while. That is precisely the case here. I think I should recognize your man if I were to see him."

"Well," said Farrar, "here's your chance."

The company outside were moving in. Two or three of the older ladies came first, carrying their wraps; then a troop of girls, among whom was Miss Trevor; and lastly, a man. Farrar and I had walked to the door while the women turned into the drawing-room, so that we were brought face to face with him, suddenly. At sight of me he halted abruptly, as though he had struck the edge of a door, changed color, and held out his hand, tentatively. Then he withdrew it again, for I made no sign of recognition.

It was the Celebrity!

I felt a shock of disgust as I passed out. Masquerading, it must be admitted, is not pleasant to the taste; and the whole farce, as it flashed through my mind, - his advertised trip, his turning up here under an assumed name, had an ill savor. Perhaps some of the things they said of him might be true, after all.

"Who the devil is he?" said Farrar, dropping for once his indifference; "he looked as if he knew you."

I evaded.

"He may have taken me for some one else," I answered with all the coolness I could muster. "I have never met any one of his name. His voice and handwriting, however, are very much like those of a man I used to know."

Farrar was very poor company that evening, and left me early. I went to my rooms and had taken down a volume of Carlyle, who can generally command my attention, when there came a knock at the door.

"Come in," I replied, with an instinctive sense of prophecy.

This was fulfilled at once by the appearance of the Celebrity. He was attired - for the details of his dress forced themselves upon me vividly - in a rough-spun suit of knickerbockers, a colored-shirt having a large and prominent gold stud, red and brown stockings of a diamond pattern, and heavy walking-boots. And he entered with an air of assurance that was maddening.

"My dear Crocker," he exclaimed, "you have no idea how delighted I am to see you here!"

I rose, first placing a book-mark in Carlyle, and assured him that I was surprised to see him here.

"Surprised to see me!" he returned, far from being damped by my manner. "In fact, I am a little surprised to see myself here."

He sank back on the window-seat and clasped his hands behind his head.

"But first let me thank you for respecting my

incognito," he said.

I tried hard to keep my temper, marvelling at the ready way he had chosen to turn my action.

"And now," he continued, "I suppose you want to know why I came out here." He easily supplied the lack of cordial solicitation on my part.

"Yes, I should like to know," I said.

Thus having aroused my curiosity, he took his time about appeasing it, after the custom of his kind. He produced a gold cigarette case, offered me a cigarette, which I refused, took one himself and blew the smoke in rings toward the ceiling. Then, raising himself on his elbow, he drew his features together in such a way as to lead me to believe he was about to impart some valuable information.

"Crocker," said he, "it's the very deuce to be famous, isn't it?"

"I suppose it is," I replied curtly, wondering what he was driving at; "I have never tried it."

"An ordinary man, such as you, can't conceive of the torture a fellow in my position is obliged to go through the year round, but especially in the summer, when one wishes to go off on a rest. You know what I mean, of course."

"I am afraid I do not," I answered, in a vain endeavor to embarrass him.

"You're thicker than when I used to know you, then,"

he returned with candor. "To tell the truth, Crocker, I often wish I were back at the law, and had never written a line. I am paying the penalty of fame. Wherever I go I am hounded to death by the people who have read my books, and they want to dine and wine me for the sake of showing me off at their houses. I am heartily sick and tired of it all; you would be if you had to go through it. I could stand a winter, but the worst comes in the summer, when one meets the women who fire all sorts of socio-psychological questions at one for solution, and who have suggestions for stories." He shuddered.

"And what has all this to do with your coming here?" I cut in, strangling a smile.

He twisted his cigarette at an acute angle with his face, and looked at me out of the corner of his eye.

"I'll try to be a little plainer," he went on, sighing as one unused to deal with people who require crosses on their t's. "I've been worried almost out of my mind with attention - nothing but attention the whole time. I can't go on the street but what I'm stared at and pointed out, so I thought of a scheme to relieve it for a time. It was becoming unbearable. I determined to assume a name and go to some quiet little place for the summer, West, if possible, where I was not likely to be recognized, and have three months of rest."

He paused, but I offered no comment.

"Well, the more I thought of it, the better I liked the idea. I met a western man at the club and asked him about western resorts, quiet ones. 'Have you heard of Asquith?' says he. 'No,' said I; 'describe it.' He did, and it was just the place; quaint, restful, and retired. Of course I put him off the track, but I did not count on striking you. My man boxed up, and we were off in twenty-four hours, and here I am."

Now all this was very fine, but not at all in keeping with the Celebrity's character as I had come to conceive it. The idea that adulation ever cloyed on him was ludicrous in itself. In fact I thought the whole story fishy, and came very near to saying so.

"You won't tell anyone who I am, will you?" he asked anxiously.

He even misinterpreted my silences.

"Certainly not," I replied. "It is no concern of mine. You might come here as Emil Zola or Ralph Waldo Emerson and it would make no difference to me."

He looked at me dubiously, even suspiciously.

"That's a good chap," said he, and was gone, leaving me to reflect on the ways of genius.

And the longer I reflected, the more positive I became that there existed a more potent reason for the Celebrity's disguise than ennui. As actions speak louder than words, so does a man's character often give the lie to his tongue.

CHAPTER IV

A Lion in an ass's skin is still a lion in spite of his disguise. Conversely, the same might be said of an ass in a lion's skin. The Celebrity ran after women with the same readiness and helplessness that a dog will chase chickens, or that a stream will run down hill. Women differ from chickens, however, in the fact that they find pleasure in being chased by a certain kind of a man. The Celebrity was this kind of a man. From the moment his valet deposited his luggage in his rooms, Charles Wrexell Allen became the social hero of Asquith. It is by straws we are enabled to tell which way the wind is blowing, and I first noticed his partiality for Miss Trevor from the absence of the lively conflicts she was wont to have with Farrar. These ceased entirely after the Celebrity's arrival. It was the latter who now commanded the conversation at our table.

I was truly sorry for Farrar, for I knew the man, the depth of his nature, and the scope of the shock. He carried it off altogether too well, and both the studied lightness of his actions and the increased carelessness of his manner made me fear that what before was feigned, might turn to a real bitterness.

For Farrar's sake, if the Celebrity had been content with women in general, all would have been well; but he was unable to generalize, in one sense, and to particularize, in another. And it was plain that he wished to monopolize Miss Trevor, while still retaining a hold upon the others. For my sake, had he been content with women alone, I should have had no cause to complain. But it seemed that I had an attraction for him, second only to women, which I could not account for. And I began to be cursed with a great deal of his company. Since he was absolutely impervious to hints, and would not take no for an answer, I was helpless. When he had no engagement he would thrust himself on me. He seemed to know by intuition - for I am very sure I never told him - what my amusement was to be the mornings I did not go to the county-seat, and he would invariably turn up, properly equipped, as I was making my way with judge Short to the tennis court, or carrying my oars to the water. It was in vain that I resorted to subterfuge: that I went to bed early intending to be away before the Celebrity's rising hour. I found he had no particular rising hour. No matter how early I came down, I would find him on the veranda, smoking cigarettes, or otherwise his man would be there with a message to say that his master would shortly join me if I would kindly wait. And at last I began to realize in my harassed soul that all elusion was futile, and to take such holidays as I could get, when he was off with a girl, in a spirit of thankfulness.

Much of this persecution I might have put up with, indeed, had I not heard, in one way or another, that he was doing me the honor of calling me his intimate. This I could not stand, and I soberly resolved to leave Asquith and go back to town, which I should indeed have done if deliverance had not arrived from an unexpected quarter.

One morning I had been driven to the precarious refuge afforded by the steps of the inn, after rejecting offers from the Celebrity to join him in a variety of amusements. But even here I was not free from interruption, for he was seated on a horse-block below me, playing with a fox terrier. Judge Short had gone to town, and Farrar was off for a three days' cruise up the lake. I was bitterly regretting I had not gone with him when the distant notes of a coach horn reached my ear, and I descried a four-in-hand winding its way up the inn road from the direction of Mohair.

"That must be your friend Cooke," remarked the Celebrity, looking up.

There could be no doubt of it. With little difficulty I recognized on the box the familiar figure of my first important client, and beside him was a lady whom I supposed to be Mrs. Farquhar Fenelon Cooke, although I had had no previous knowledge that such a person existed. The horses were on a brisk trot, and Mr. Cooke seemed to be getting the best out of them for the benefit of the sprinkling of people on the inn porch. Indeed, I could not but admire the dexterous turn of the wrist which served Mr. Cooke to swing his leaders into the circle and up the hill, while the liveried guard leaned far out in anticipation of a stumble. Mr. Cooke hailed me with a beaming smile and a flourish of the whip as he drew up and descended from the box.

"Maria," he exclaimed, giving me a hearty grip, "this is the man that won Mohair. My wife, Crocker."

I was somewhat annoyed at this effusiveness before the Celebrity, but I looked up and caught Mrs. Cooke's eye. It was the calm eye of a general.

"I am glad of the opportunity to thank you, Mr. Crocker," she said simply. And I liked her from that moment.

Mr. Cooke at once began a tirade against the residents of Asquith for permitting a sandy and generally disgraceful condition of the roads. So roundly did he vituperate the inn management in particular, and with such a loud flow of words, that I trembled lest he should be heard on the veranda. The Celebrity stood by the block, in an amazement which gave me a wicked pleasure, and it was some minutes before I had the chance to introduce him.

Mr. Cooke's idea of an introduction, however, was no mere word-formula: it was fraught with a deeper and a bibulous meaning. He presented the Celebrity to his wife, and then invited both of us to go inside with him by one of those neat and cordial paraphrases in which he was skilled. I preferred to remain with Mrs. Cooke, and it was with a gleam of hope at a possible deliverance from my late persecution that I watched the two disappear together through the hall and into the smoking-room.

"How do you like Mohair?" I asked Mrs. Cooke.

"Do you mean the house or the park?" she laughed; and then, seeing my embarrassment, she went on: "Oh, the house is just like everything else Fenelon meddles with. Outside it's a mixture of all the styles, and inside a hash of all the nationalities from Siamese to Spanish. Fenelon hangs the Oriental tinsels he has collected on pieces of black baronial oak, and the coat-of-arms he had designed by our Philadelphia jewellers is stamped on the dining-room chairs, and even worked into the fire screens."

There was nothing paltry in her criticism of her husband, nothing she would not have said to his face. She was a woman who made you feel this, for sincerity was written all over her. I could not help wondering why she gave Mr. Cooke line in the matter of household decoration, unless it was that he considered Mohair his own, private hobby, and that she humored him. Mrs. Cooke was not without tact, and I have no doubt she perceived my reluctance to talk about her husband and respected it.

"We drove down to bring you back to luncheon," she said.

I thanked her and accepted. She was curious to hear about Asquith and its people, and I told her all I knew.

"I should like to meet some of them," she explained, "for we intend having a cotillon at Mohair, - a kind of house-warming, you know. A party of Mr. Cooke's friends is coming out for it in his car, and he thought something of inviting the people of Asquith up for a dance."

I had my doubts concerning the wisdom of an entertainment, the success of which depended on the fusion of a party of Mr. Cooke's friends and a company from Asquith. But I held my peace. She shot a question at me suddenly:

"Who is this Mr. Allen?"

"He registers from Boston, and only came a fortnight ago," I replied vaguely.

"He doesn't look quite right; as though he had been set down on the wrong planet, you know," said Mrs. Cooke, her finger on her temple. "What is he like?"

"Well," I answered, at first with uncertainty, then with inspiration, "he would do splendidly to lead your cotillon, if you think of having one."

"So you do not dance, Mr. Crocker?"

I was somewhat set back by her perspicuity.

"No, I do not," said I.

"I thought not," she said, laughing. It must have been my expression which prompted her next remark.

"I was not making fun of you," she said, more soberly; "I do not like Mr. Allen any better than you do, and I have only seen him once."

"But I have not said I did not like him," I objected.

"Of course not," said Mrs. Cooke, quizzically.

At that moment, to my relief, I discerned the Celebrity and Mr. Cooke in the hallway.

"Here they come, now," she went on. "I do wish Fenelon would keep his hands off the people he meets. I can feel he is going to make an intimate of that man. Mark my words, Mr. Crocker."

I not only marked them, I prayed for their fulfilment.

There was that in Mr. Cooke which, for want of a

better name, I will call instinct. As he came down the steps, his arm linked in that of the Celebrity, his attitude towards his wife was both apologetic and defiant. He had at once the air of a child caught with a forbidden toy, and that of a stripling of twenty-one who flaunts a cigar in his father's face.

"Maria," he said, "Mr. Allen has consented to come back with us for lunch."

We drove back to Mohair, Mr. Cooke and the Celebrity on the box, Mrs. Cooke and I behind. Except to visit the boathouses I had not been to Mohair since the day of its completion, and now the full beauty of the approach struck me for the first time. We swung by the lodge, the keeper holding open the iron gate as we passed, and into the wide driveway, hewn, as it were, out of the virgin forest. The sandy soil had been strengthened by a deep road-bed of clay imported from the interior, which was spread in turn with a fine gravel, which crunched under the heavy wheels. From the lodge to the house, a full mile, branches had been pruned to let the sunshine sift through in splotches, but the wild nature of the place had been skilfully retained. We curved hither and thither under the giant trees until suddenly, as a whip straightens in the snapping, one of the ancient tribes of the forest might have sent an arrow down the leafy gallery into the open, and at the far end we caught sight of the palace framed in the vista. It was a triumph for Farrar, and I wished that the palace had been more worthy.

The Celebrity did not stint his praises of Mohair, coming up the drive, but so lavish were his comments on the house that they won for him a lasting place in Mr. Cooke's affections, and encouraged my client to pull up his horses in a favorable spot, and expand on the beauties of the mansion.

"Taking it altogether," said he, complacently, "it is rather a neat box, and I let myself loose on it. I had all these ideas I gathered knocking about the world, and I gave them to Willis, of Philadelphia, to put together for me. But he's honest enough not to claim the house. Take, for instance, that minaret business on the west; I picked that up from a mosque in Algiers. The oriel just this side is whole cloth from Haddon Hall, and the galleried porch next it from a Florentine villa. The conical capped tower I got from a French chateau, and some of the features on the south from a Buddhist temple in Japan. Only a little blending and grouping was necessary, and Willis calls himself an architect, and wasn't equal to it. Now," he added, "get the effect. Did you ever see another house like it?"

"Magnificent!" exclaimed the Celebrity.

"And then," my client continued, warming under this generous appreciation, "there's something very smart about those colors. They're my racing colors. Of course the granite's a little off, but it isn't prominent. Willis kicked hard when it came to painting the oriel yellow, but an architect always takes it for granted he knows it all, and a - "

"Fenelon," said Mrs. Cooke, "luncheon is waiting."

Mrs. Cooke dominated at luncheon and retired, and it is certain that both Mr. Cooke and the Celebrity breathed more freely when she had gone. If her criticisms on the exterior of the house were just, those on the interior were more so. Not only did I find the coat-of-arms set forth on the chairs, fire-screens, and other prominent articles, but it was even cut into the swinging door of the butler's pantry. The motto I am afraid my client never took the trouble to have translated, and I am inclined to think his jewellers put up a little joke on him when they chose it. "Be Sober and Boast not."

I observed that Mrs. Cooke, when she chose, could exert the subduing effect on her husband of a soft pedal on a piano; and during luncheon she kept, the soft pedal on. And the Celebrity, being in some degree a kindred spirit, was also held in check. But his wife had no sooner left the room when Mr. Cooke began on the subject uppermost in his mind. I had suspected that his trip to Asquith that morning was for a purpose at which Mrs. Cooke had hinted. But she, with a woman's tact, had aimed to accomplish by degrees that which her husband would carry by storm.

"You've been at Asquith sometime, Crocker," Mr. Cooke began, "long enough to know the people."

"I know some of them," I said guardedly. But the rush was not to be stemmed.

"How many do you think you can muster for that entertainment of mine? Fifty? I ought to have fifty, at least. Suppose you pick out fifty, and send me up the names. I want good lively ones, you understand, that will stir things up."

"I am afraid there are not fifty of that kind there," I replied.

His face fell, but brightened again instantly. He

appealed to the Celebrity.

"How about it, old man?" said he.

The Celebrity answered, with becoming modesty, that the Asquithians were benighted. They had never had any one to show them how to enjoy life. But there was hope for them.

"That's it," exclaimed my client, slapping his thigh, and turning triumphantly to me, he continued, "You're all right, Crocker, and know enough to win a damned big suit, but you're not the man to steer a delicate thing of this kind."

This is how, to my infinite relief, the Celebrity came to engineer the matter of the housewarming; and to him it was much more congenial. He accepted the task cheerfully, and went about it in such a manner as to leave no doubt in my mind as to its ultimate success. He was a master hand at just such problems, and this one had a double attraction. It pleased him to be thought the arbiter of such a worthy cause, while he acquired a prominence at Asquith which satisfied in some part a craving which he found inseparable from incognito.

His tactics were worthy of a skilled diplomatist. Before we left Mohair that day he had exacted as a condition that Mr. Cooke should not appear at the inn or in its vicinity until after the entertainment. To this my client readily pledged himself with that absolute freedom from suspicion which formed one of the most admirable traits of his character. The Celebrity, being intuitively quick where women were concerned, had surmised that Mrs. Cooke did not like him; but as her interests in the affair of the cotillon coincided with those of Mr. Cooke, she was available as a means to an end. The Celebrity deemed her, from a social standpoint, decidedly the better part of the Mohair establishment, and he contrived, by a system of manoeuvres I failed to grasp, to throw her forward while he kept Mr. Cooke in the background.

He had much to contend with; above all, an antecedent prejudice against the Cookes, in reality a prejudice against the world, the flesh, and the devil, natural to any quiet community, and of which Mohair and its appurtenances were taken as the outward and visible signs. Older people came to Asquith for simplicity and rest, and the younger ones were brought there for these things. Nearly all had sufficient wealth to seek, if they chose, gayety and ostentation at the eastern resorts. But Asquithians held gayety and ostentation at a discount, and maintained there was gayety enough at home.

If any one were fitted to overcome this prejudice, it was Mrs. Cooke. Her tastes and manners were as simple as her gowns. The Celebrity, by arts unknown, induced Mrs. Judge Short and two other ladies to call at Mohair on a certain afternoon when Mr. Cooke was trying a trotter on the track. The three returned wondering and charmed with Mrs. Cooke; they were sure she had had no hand in the furnishing of that atrocious house. Their example was followed by others at a time when the master of Mohair was superintending in person the docking of some two-year-olds, and equally invisible. These ladies likewise came back to sing Mrs. Cooke's praises. Mrs. Cooke returned the calls. She took tea on the inn veranda, and drove Mrs. Short around Mohair in her victoria. Mr. Cooke being seen only on rare and fleeting occasions, there gradually got abroad a most curious misconception of that gentleman's character, while over his personality floated a mist of legend which the Celebrity took good care not to dispel. Farrar, who despised nonsense, was ironical and non-committal when appealed to, and certainly I betrayed none of my client's attributes. Hence it came that Asquith, before the house-warming, knew as little about Farquhar Fenelon Cooke, the man, as the nineteenth century knows about William Shakespeare, and was every whit as curious. Like Shakespeare, Mr. Cooke was judged by his works, and from these he was generally conceded to be an illiterate and indifferent person of barbarous tastes and a mania for horses. He was further described as ungentlemanly by a brace of spinsters who had been within earshot on the veranda the morning he had abused the Asquith roads, but their evidence was not looked upon as damning. That Mr. Cooke would appear at the cotillon never entered any one's head.

Thus it was, for a fortnight, Mr. Cooke maintained a most rigid seclusion. Would that he had discovered in the shroud of mystery the cloak of fame!

VOLUME 2.

CHAPTER V

It was small wonder, said the knowing at Asquith, that
Mr. Charles Wrexell Allen should be attracted by Irene
Trevor. With the lake breezes of the north the red and
the tan came into her cheeks, those boon companions
of the open who are best won by the water-winds.
Perhaps they brought, too, the spring to the step and
the light under the long lashes when she flashed a look
across the table. Little by little it became plain that
Miss Trevor was gaining ground with the Celebrity to
the neglect of the other young women at Asquith, and
when it was announced that he was to lead the cotillon
with her, the fact was regarded as significant. Even at
Asquith such things were talked about. Mr. Allen
became a topic and a matter of conjecture. He was, I
believe, generally regarded as a good match; his
unimpeachable man-servant argued worldly posse-
ssions, of which other indications were not lacking,
while his crest was cited as a material sign of family.
Yet when Miss Brewster, one of the brace of spinsters,
who hailed from Brookline and purported to be an up-
to-date edition of the Boston Blue Book, questioned
the Celebrity on this vital point after the searching
manner warranted by the gravity of the subject, he was
unable to acquit himself satisfactorily. When this
conversation was repeated in detail within the hearing

of the father of the young woman in question, and undoubtedly for his benefit, Mr. Trevor threw shame to the winds and scandalized the Misses Brewster then and there by proclaiming his father to have been a country storekeeper. In the eyes of Mr. Farquhar Fenelon Cooke the apotheosis of the Celebrity was complete. The people of Asquith were not only willing to attend the house-warming, but had been worked up to the pitch of eagerness. The Celebrity as a matter of course was master of ceremonies. He originated the figures and arranged the couples, of which there were twelve from Asquith and ten additional young women. These ten were assigned to the ten young men whom Mr. Cooke expected in his private car, and whose appearances, heights, and temperaments the Celebrity obtained from Mr. Cooke, carefully noted, and compared with those of the young women. Be it said in passing that Mrs. Cooke had nothing to do with any of it, but exhibited an almost criminal indifference. Mr. Cooke had even chosen the favors; charity forbids that I should say what they were.

Owing to the frequent consultations which these preparations made necessary the Celebrity was much in the company of my client, which he came greatly to prefer to mine, and I therefore abandoned my determination to leave Asquith. I was settling down delightedly to my old, easy, and unmolested existence when Farrar and I received an invitation, which amounted to a summons, to go to Mohair and make ourselves generally useful. So we packed up and went. We made an odd party before the arrival of the Ten, particularly when the Celebrity dropped in for lunch or dinner. He could not be induced to remain permanently at Mohair because Miss Trevor was at Asquith, but he appropriated a Hempstead cart from the Mohair stables and made the trip sometimes twice in a day. The fact that Mrs. Cooke treated him with unqualified disapproval did not dampen his spirits or lessen the frequency of his visits, nor, indeed, did it seem to create any breach between husband and wife. Mr. Cooke took it for granted that his friends should not please his wife, and Mrs. Cooke remarked to Farrar and me that her husband was old enough to know better, and too old to be taught. She loved him devotedly and showed it in a hundred ways, but she was absolutely incapable of dissimulation.

Thanks to Mrs. Cooke, our visit to Mohair was a pleasant one. We were able in many ways to help in the arrangements, especially Farrar, who had charge of decorating the grounds. We saw but little of Mr. Cooke and the Celebrity.

The arrival of the Ten was an event of importance, and occurred the day of the dance. I shall treat the Ten as a whole because they did not materially differ from one another in dress or habits or ambition or general usefulness on this earth. It is true that Mr. Cooke had been able to make delicate distinctions between them for the aid of the Celebrity, but such distinctions were beyond me, and the power to make them lay only in a long and careful study of the species which I could not afford to give. Likewise the life of any one of the Ten was the life of all, and might be truthfully represented by a single year, since each year was exactly like the preceding. The ordinary year, as is well-known, begins on the first of January. But theirs was not the ordinary year, nor the Church year, nor the fiscal year. Theirs began in the Fall with the New York Horse Show. And I am of the opinion, though open to correction, that they dated from the first Horse Show instead of from the birth of Christ. It is certain that they were much better versed in the history of the Association than in that of the Union, in the biography of Excelsior rather than that of Lincoln. The Dog Show was another event to which they looked forward, when they migrated to New York and put up at the country places of their friends. But why go farther?

The Ten made themselves very much at home at Mohair. One of them told the Celebrity he reminded him very much of a man he had met in New York and who had written a book, or something of that sort, which made the Celebrity wince. The afternoon was spent in one of the stable lofts, where Mr. Cooke had set up a mysterious L-shaped box, in one arm of which a badger was placed by a groom, while my client's Sarah, a terrier, was sent into the other arm to invite the badger out. His objections exceeded the highest hopes; he dug his claws into the wood and devoted himself to Sarah's countenance with unremitting industry. This occupation was found so absorbing that it was with difficulty the Ten were induced to abandon it and dress for an early dinner, and only did so after the second peremptory message from Mrs. Cooke.

"It's always this way," said Mr. Cooke, regretfully, as he watched Sarah licking the accessible furrows in her face; "I never started in on anything worth doing yet that Maria did not stop it."

Farrar and I were not available for the dance, and after dinner we looked about for a quiet spot in which to weather it, and where we could be within reach if needed. Such a place as this was the Florentine galleried porch, which ran along outside the upper windows of the ball-room; these were flung open, for the night was warm. At one end of the room the musicians, imported from Minneapolis by Mr. Cooke, were striking the first discordant notes of the tuning, while at the other the Celebrity and my client, in scarlet hunting-coats, were gravely instructing the Ten, likewise in scarlet hunting-coats, as to their conduct and functions. We were reviewing these interesting proceedings when Mrs. Cooke came hurrying towards us. She held a letter in her hand.

"You know," said she, "that Mr. Cooke is forgetful, particularly when his mind is occupied with important matters, as it has been for some time. Here is a letter from my niece, Miss Thorn, which he has carried in his pocket since Monday. We expected her two weeks ago, and had given her up. But it seems she was to leave Philadelphia on Wednesday, and will be at that forlorn little station of Asquith at half-past nine to-night. I want you two to go over and meet her."

We expressed our readiness, and in ten minutes were in the station wagon, rolling rapidly down the long drive, for it was then after nine. We passed on the way the van of the guests from Asquith. As we reached the lodge we heard the whistle, and we backed up against one side of the platform as the train pulled up at the other.

Farrar and I are not imaginative; we did not picture to ourselves any particular type for the girl we were going to meet, we were simply doing our best to get to the station before the train. We jumped from the wagon and were watching the people file out of the car, and I noticed that more than one paused to look back over their shoulders as they reached the door. Then came a maid with hand-bag and shawls, and after her a tall young lady. She stood for a moment holding her skirt above the grimy steps, with something of the stately pose which Richter has given his Queen Louise on the stairway, and the light of the reflector fell full upon her. She looked around expectantly, and recognizing Mrs. Cooke's maid, who had stepped forward to relieve hers of the shawls, Miss Thorn greeted her with a smile which greatly prepossessed us in her favor.

"How do you do, Jennie?" she said. "Did any one else come?"

"Yes, Miss Marian," replied Jennie, abashed but pleased, - "these gentlemen."

Farrar and I introduced ourselves, awkwardly enough, and we both tried to explain at once how it was that neither Mr. nor Mrs. Cooke was there to meet her. Of course we made an absolute failure of it. She scanned our faces with a puzzled expression for a while and then broke into a laugh.

"I think I understand," she said; "they are having the house-warming."

"She's first-rate at guessing," said Farrar to me as we fled precipitately to see that the trunks were hoisted into the basket. Neither of us had much presence of mind as we climbed into the wagon, and, what was even stranger, could not account for the lack of it. Miss Thorn was seated in the corner; in spite of the darkness I could see that she was laughing at us still.

"I feel very badly that I should have taken you away from the dance," we heard her say.

"We don't dance," I answered clumsily, "and we were glad to come."

"Yes, we were glad to come," Farrar chimed in.

Then we relapsed into a discomfited silence, and wished we were anywhere else. But Miss Thorn relieved the situation by laughing aloud, and with such a hearty enjoyment that instead of getting angry and more mortified we began to laugh ourselves, and instantly felt better. After that we got along famously. She had at once the air of good fellowship and the dignity of a woman, and she seemed to understand Farrar and me perfectly. Not once did she take us over our heads, though she might have done so with ease, and we knew this and were thankful. We began to tell her about Mohair and the cotillon, and of our point of observation from the Florentine galleried porch, and she insisted she would join us there. By the time we reached the house we were thanking our stars she had come. Mrs. Cooke came out under the port-cochere to welcome her.

"Unfortunately there is no one to dance with you, Marian," she said; "but if I had not by chance gone through your uncle's pockets, there would have been no one to meet you."

I think I had never felt my deficiency in dancing until that moment. But Miss Thorn took her aunt's hand affectionately in hers.

"My dear Aunt Maria," said she, "I would not dance to-night if there were twenty to choose from. I should like nothing better than to look on with these two. We are the best of friends already," she added, turning towards us, "are we not?"

"We are indeed," we hastened to assure her.

Mrs. Cooke smiled.

"You should have been a man, Marian," she said as they went upstairs together.

We made our way to the galleried porch and sat down, there being a lull in the figures just then. We each took out a cigar and lighted a match; and then looked across at the other. We solemnly blew our matches out.

"Perhaps she doesn't like smoke," said Farrar, voicing the sentiment.

"Perhaps not," said I.

Silence.

"I wonder how she will get along with the Ten?" I queried.

"Better than with us," he answered in his usual strain. "They're trained."

"Or with Allen?" I added irresistibly.

"Women are all alike," said Farrar.

At this juncture Miss Thorn herself appeared at the end of the gallery, her shoulders wrapped in a gray cape trimmed with fur. She stood regarding us with some amusement as we rose to receive her.

"Light your cigars and be sensible," said she, "or I shall go in."

We obeyed. The three of us turned to the window to watch the figure, the music of which was just beginning. Mr. Cooke, with the air of an English squire at his own hunt ball, was strutting contentedly up and down one end of the room, now pausing to exchange a few hearty words with some Presbyterian matron from Asquith, now to congratulate Mr. Trevor on the appearance of his daughter. Lined against the opposite wall were the Celebrity and his ten red-coated followers, just rising for the figure. It was very plain that Miss Trevor was radiantly happy; she was easily the handsomest girl in the room, and I could not help philosophizing when I saw her looking up into the Celebrity's eyes upon the seeming inconsistency of nature, who has armed and warned woman against all but her most dangerous enemy.

And then a curious thing happened. The Celebrity, as if moved by a sudden uncontrollable impulse, raised his eyes until they rested on the window in which we were. Although his dancing was perfect, he lost the step without apparent cause, his expression changed, and for the moment he seemed to be utterly confused. But only for the moment; in a trice he had caught the time again and swept Miss Trevor rapidly down the room and out of sight. I looked instinctively at the girl beside me. She had thrown her head forward, and in the streaming light I saw that her lips were parted in a smile.

I resolved upon a stroke.

"Mr. Allen," I remarked, "leads admirably."

"Mr. Allen!" she exclaimed, turning on me.

"Yes, it is Mr. Allen who is leading," I repeated.

An expression of perplexity spread over her face, but she said nothing. My curiosity was aroused to a high pitch, and questions were rising to my lips which I repressed with difficulty. For Miss Thorn had displayed, purposely or not, a reticence which my short acquaintance with her compelled me to respect; and, besides, I was bound by a promise not to betray the Celebrity's secret. I was, however, convinced from what had occurred that she had met the Celebrity in the East, and perhaps known him.

Had she fallen in love with him, as was the common fate of all young women he met? I changed my opinion on this subject a dozen times. Now I was sure, as I looked at her, that she was far too sensible; again, a doubt would cross my mind as the Celebrity himself would cross my view, the girl on his arm reduced to adoration. I followed him narrowly when in sight. Miss Thorn was watching him, too, her eyes half closed, as though in thought. But beyond the fact that he threw himself into the dance with a somewhat increased fervor, perhaps, his manner betokened no uneasiness, and not even by a glance did he betray any disturbing influence from above.

Thus we stood silently until the figure was finished, when Miss Thorn seated herself in one of the wicker chairs behind us.

"Doesn't it make you wish to dance?" said Farrar to her. "It is hard luck you should be doomed to spend the evening with two such useless fellows as we are."

She did not catch his remark at first, as was natural in a person preoccupied. Then she bit her lips to repress a smile.

"I assure you, Mr. Farrar," she said with force, "I have never in my life wished to dance as little as I do now."

But a voice interrupted her, and the scarlet coat of the Celebrity was thrust into the light between us. Farrar excused himself abruptly and disappeared.

"Never wished to dance less!" cried the Celebrity. "Upon my word, Miss Thorn, that's too bad. I came up to ask you to reconsider your determination, as one of the girls from Asquith is leaving, and there is an extra man."

"You are very kind," said Miss Thorn, quietly, "but I prefer to remain here."

My surmise, then, was correct. She had evidently met the Celebrity, and there was that in his manner of addressing her, without any formal greeting, which seemed to point to a close acquaintance.

"You know Mr. Allen, then, Miss Thorn?" said I.

"What can you mean?" she exclaimed, wheeling on me; "this is not Mr. Allen."

"Hang you, Crocker," the Celebrity put in impatiently; "Miss Thorn knows who I am as well as you do."

"I confess it is a little puzzling," said she; "perhaps it is because I am tired from travelling, and my brain refuses to work. But why in the name of all that is strange do you call him Mr. Allen?"

The Celebrity threw himself into the chair beside her and asked permission to light a cigarette.

"I am going to ask you the favor of respecting my incognito, Miss Thorn, as Crocker has done," he said. "Crocker knew me in the East, too. I had not counted upon finding him at Asquith."

Miss Thorn straightened herself and made a gesture of impatience.

"An incognito!" she cried. "But you have taken another man's name. And you already had his face and figure!"

I jumped.

"That is so," he calmly returned; "the name was ready to hand, and so I took it. I don't imagine it will make any difference to him. It's only a whim of mine, and with me there's no accounting for a whim. I make it a point to gratify every one that strikes me. I confess to being eccentric, you know."

"You must get an enormous amount of gratification out of this," she said dryly. "What if the other man should happen along?"

"Scarcely at Asquith."

"I have known stranger things to occur," said she.

The Celebrity smiled and smoked.

"I'll wager, now," he went on, "that you little thought

to find me here incognito. But it is delicious, I assure you, to lead once more a commonplace and unmolested existence."

"Delightful," said Miss Thorn.

"People never consider an author apart from his work, you know, and I confess I had a desire to find out how I would get along. And there comes a time when a man wishes he had never written a book, and a longing to be sought after for his own sake and to be judged on his own merits. And then it is a great relief to feel that one is not at the beck and call of any one and every one wherever one goes, and to know that one is free to choose one's own companions and do as one wishes."

"The sentiment is good," Miss Thorn agreed, "very good. But doesn't it seem a little odd, Mr. Crocker," she continued, appealing to me, "that a man should take the pains to advertise a trip to Europe in order to gratify a whim of this sort?"

"It is indeed incomprehensible to me," I replied, with a kind of grim pleasure, "but you must remember that I have always led a commonplace existence."

Although the Celebrity was almost impervious to sarcasm, he was now beginning to exhibit visible signs of uneasiness, the consciousness dawning upon him that his eccentricity was not receiving the ovation it merited. It was with a palpable relief that he heard the first warning notes of the figure.

"Am I to understand that you wish me to do my part in concealing your identity?" asked Miss Thorn, cutting him short as he was expressing pleasure at her arrival.

"If you will be so kind," he answered, and departed with a bow. There was a mischievous mirth in her eye as she took her place in the window. Below in the ball-room sat Miss Trevor surrounded by men, and I saw her face lighting at the Celebrity's approach.

"Who is that beautiful girl he is dancing with?" said Miss Thorn.

I told her.

"Have you read his books?" she asked, after a pause.

"Some of them."

"So have I"

The Celebrity was not mentioned again that evening.

CHAPTER VI

As an endeavor to unite Mohair and Asquith the cotillon had proved a dismal failure. They were as the clay and the brass. The next morning Asquith was split into factions and rent by civil strife, and the porch of the inn was covered by little knots of women, all trying to talk at once; their faces told an ominous tale. Not a man was to be seen. The Minneapolis, St. Paul, and Chicago papers, all of which had previously contained elaborate illustrated accounts of Mr. Cooke's palatial park and residence, came out that morning bristling with headlines about the ball, incidentally holding up the residents of a quiet and retiring little community in a light that scandalized them beyond measure. And Mr. Charles Wrexell Allen, treasurer of the widely known Miles Standish Bicycle Company, was said to have led the cotillon in a manner that left nothing to be desired.

So it was this gentleman whom the Celebrity was personating! A queer whim indeed.

After that, I doubt if the court of Charles the Second was regarded by the Puritans with a greater abhorrence than was Mohair by the good ladies of Asquith. Mr. Cooke and his ten friends were branded as profligates whose very scarlet coats bore witness that they were of the devil. Mr. Cooke himself, who particularly savored of brimstone, would much better have remained behind the arras, for he was denounced with such energy and bitterness that those who might have attempted his defence were silent, and their very silence told against them. Mr. Cooke had indeed outdone himself in hospitality. He had posted punch-bowls in every available corner, and so industriously did he devote himself to the duties of host, as he conceived them, that as many as four of the patriarchs of Asquith and pillars of the church had returned home more or less insensible, while others were quite incoherent. The odds being overwhelming, the master of Mohair had at length fallen a victim to his own good cheer. He took post with Judge Short at the foot of the stair, where, in spite of the protests of the Celebrity and of other well-disposed persons, the two favored the parting guests with an occasional impromptu song and waved genial good-byes to the ladies. And, when Mrs. Short attempted to walk by with her head in the air, as though the judge were in an adjoining county, he so far forgot his judicial dignity as to chuck her under the chin, an act which was applauded with much boyish delight by Mr. Cooke, and a remark which it is just as well not to repeat. The judge desired to spend the night at Mohair, but was afterwards taken home by main force, and the next day his meals were brought up to him. It is small wonder that Mrs. Short was looked upon as the head of the outraged party. The Ten were only spoken of in whispers. Three of them had been unable to come to time when the last figure was called, whereupon their partners were whisked off the scene without so much as being allowed to pay their respects to the hostess. Besides these offences, there were other minor barbarisms too numerous to mention.

Although Mrs. Short's party was all-powerful at Asquith, there were some who, for various reasons, refused to agree in the condemnation of Mr. Cooke. Judge Short and the other gentlemen in his position were, of course, restricted, but Mr. Trevor came out boldly in the face of severe criticism and declared that his daughter should accept any invitation from Mrs. Cooke that she chose, and paid but little attention to the coolness resulting therefrom. He was fast getting a reputation for oddity. And the Celebrity tried to conciliate both parties, and succeeded, though none but he could have done it. At first he was eyed with suspicion and disgust as he drove off to Mohair in his Hempstead cart, and was called many hard names. But he had a way about him which won them in the end.

A few days later I ran over to Mohair and found my client with the colored Sunday supplement of a Chicago newspaper spread out before him, eyeing the page with something akin to childish delight. I discovered that it was a picture of his own hunt ball, and as a bit of color it was marvellous, the scarlet coats being very much in evidence.

"There, old man!" he exclaimed. "What do you think of that? Something of a sendoff, eh?" And he pointed to a rather stout and important gentleman in the foreground. "That's me!" he said proudly, "and they wouldn't do that for Farquhar Fenelon Cooke in Philadelphia."

"A prophet is without honor in his own country," I remarked.

"I don't set up for a prophet," said Mr. Cooke, "but I did predict that I would start a ripple here, didn't I?"

I did not deny this.

"How do I stand over there?" he inquired, designating Asquith by a twist of the head. "I hear they're acting all over the road; that they think I'm the very devil."

"Well, your stock has dropped some, I admit," I answered. "They didn't take kindly to your getting the judge drunk, you know."

"They oughtn't to complain about that," said my client; "and besides, he wasn't drunk enough to amount to anything."

"However that may be," said I, "you have the credit for leading him astray. But there is a split in your favor."

"I'm glad to know that," he said, brightening; "then I won't have to import any more."

"Any more what?" I asked.

"People from the East to keep things moving, of course. What I have here and those left me at the inn ought to be enough to run through the summer with. Don't you think so?"

I thought so, and was moving off when he called me back.

"Is the judge locked up, old man?" he demanded.

"He's under rather close surveillance," I replied, smiling.

"Crocker;" he said confidentially, "see if you can't smuggle him over here some day soon. The judge always holds good cards, and plays a number one hand."

I promised, and escaped. On the veranda I came upon Miss Thorn surrounded by some of her uncle's guests. I imagine that she was bored, for she looked it.

"Mr. Crocker," she called out, "you're just the man I have been wishing to see."

The others naturally took this for a dismissal, and she was not long in coming to her point when we were alone.

"What is it you know about this queer but gifted genius who is here so mysteriously?" she asked.

"Nothing whatever," I confessed. "I knew him before he thought of becoming a genius."

"Retrogression is always painful," she said; "but tell me something about him then."

I told her all I knew, being that narrated in these pages. "Now," said I, "if you will pardon a curiosity on my part, from what you said the other evening I inferred that he closely resembles the man whose name it pleased him to assume. And that man, I learn from the newspapers, is Mr. Charles Wrexell Allen of the 'Miles Standish Bicycle Company.'"

Miss Thorn made a comic gesture of despair.

"Why he chose Mr. Allen's name," she said, "is absolutely beyond my guessing. Unless there is some purpose behind the choice, which I do not for an instant believe, it was a foolish thing to do, and one very apt to lead to difficulties. I can understand the rest. He has a reputation for eccentricity which he feels he must keep up, and this notion of assuming a name evidently appealed to him as an inspiration."

"But why did he come out here?" I asked. "Can you tell me that?"

Miss Thorn flushed slightly, and ignored the question.

"I met the 'Celebrity,' as you call him," she said, "for the first time last winter, and I saw him frequently during the season. Of course I had heard not a little about him and his peculiarities. His name seems to have gone the length and breadth of the land. And, like most girls, I had read his books and confess I enjoyed them. It is not too much to say," she added archly, "that I made a sort of archangel out of the author."

"I can understand that," said I.

"But that did not last," she continued hastily. "I see I have got beside my story. I saw a great deal of him in New York. He came to call, and I believe I danced with him once or twice. And then my aunt, Mrs. Rivers, bought a place near Epsom, in Massachusetts, and had a house party there in May. And the Celebrity was invited."

I smiled.

"Oh, I assure you it was a mere chance," said Miss Thorn. "I mention this that I may tell you the astonishing part of it all. Epsom is one of those smoky manufacturing towns one sees in New England, and the 'Miles Standish' bicycle is made there. The day after we all arrived at my aunt's a man came up the drive on a wheel whom I greeted in a friendly way and got a decidedly uncertain bow in return.

"I thought it rather a strange shift from a marked cordiality, and spoke of the circumstance to my aunt, who was highly amused. 'Why, my dear,' said she, 'that was Mr. Allen, of the bicycle company. I was nearly deceived myself.'"

"And is the resemblance so close as that?" I exclaimed.

"So close! Believe me, they are as like as two ices from a mould. Of course, when they are together one can distinguish the Celebrity from the bicycle man. The Celebrity's chin is a little more square, and his nose straighter, and there are other little differences. I believe Mr. Allen has a slight scar on his forehead. But the likeness was remarkable, nevertheless, and it grew to be a standing joke with us. They actually dressed ludicrously alike. The Celebrity became so sensitive about it that he went back to New York before the party broke up. We grew to be quite fond of the bicycle man."

She paused and shifted her chair, which had rocked close to mine.

"And can you account for his coming to Asquith?" I asked innocently.

She was plainly embarrassed.

"I suppose I might account for it, Mr. Crocker," she replied. Then she added, with something of an impulse,

"After all, it is foolish of me not to tell you. You probably know the Celebrity well enough to have learned that he takes idiotic fancies to young women."

"Not always idiotic," I protested.

"You mean that the young women are not always idiotic, I suppose. No, not always, but nearly always. I imagine he got the idea of coming to Asquith," she went on with a change of manner, "because I chanced to mention that I was coming out here on a visit."

"Oh," I remarked, and there words failed me.

Her mouth was twitching with merriment.

"I am afraid you will have to solve the rest of it for yourself, Mr. Crocker," said she; "that is all of my contribution. My uncle tells me you are the best lawyer in the country, and I am surprised that you are so slow in getting at motives."

And I did attempt to solve it on my way back to Asquith. The conclusion I settled to, everything weighed, was this: that the Celebrity had become infatuated with Miss Thorn (I was far from blaming him for that) and had followed her first to Epsom and now to Asquith. And he had chosen to come West incognito partly through the conceit which he admitted and gloried in, and partly because he believed his prominence sufficient to obtain for him an unpleasant notoriety if he continued long enough to track the same young lady about the country. Hence he had taken the trouble to advertise a trip abroad to account for his absence. Undoubtedly his previous conquests had been made more easily, for my second talk with Miss Thorn had put my mind at rest as to her having fallen a victim to his fascinations. Her arrival at Mohair being delayed, the Celebrity had come nearly a month too soon, and in the interval that tendency of which he was the dupe still led him by the nose; he must needs make violent love to the most attractive girl on the ground, - Miss Trevor. Now that one still more attractive had arrived I was curious to see how he would steer between the two, for I made no doubt that matters had progressed rather far with Miss Trevor. And in this I was not mistaken.

But his choice of the name of Charles Wrexell Allen bothered me considerably. I finally decided that he had taken it because convenient, and because he believed Asquith to be more remote from the East than the Sandwich Islands.

Reaching the inn grounds, I climbed the hillside to a favorite haunt of mine, a huge boulder having a sloping back covered with soft turf. Hence I could watch indifferently both lake and sky. Presently, however, I was aroused by voices at the foot of the rock, and peering over the edge I discovered a kind of sewing-circle gathered there. The foliage hid me completely. I perceived the Celebrity perched upon the low branch of an apple-tree, and Miss Trevor below him, with two other girls, doing fancy-work. I shall not attempt to defend the morality of my action, but I could not get away without discovery, and the knowledge that I had heard a part of their conversation might prove disquieting to them.

The Celebrity had just published a book, under the title of 'The Sybarites', which was being everywhere discussed; and Asquith, where summer reading was general, came in for its share of the debate. Why it was called The Sybarites I have never discovered. I did not read the book because I was sick and tired of the author and his nonsense, but I imbibed, in spite of myself, something of the story and its moral from hearing it talked about. The Celebrity himself had listened to arguments on the subject with great serenity, and was nothing loth to give his opinion when appealed to. I realized at once that 'The Sybarites' was the present topic.

"Yes, it is rather an uncommon book," he was saying languidly, "but there is no use writing a story unless it is uncommon."

"Dear, how I should like to meet the author!" exclaimed a voice. "He must be a charming man, and so young, too! I believe you said you knew him, Mr. Allen."

"An old acquaintance," he answered, "and I am always reminding him that his work is overestimated."

"How can you say he is overestimated!" said a voice.

"You men are all jealous of him," said another.

"Is he handsome? I have heard he is."

"He would scarcely be called so," said the Celebrity, doubtfully.

"He is, girls," Miss Trevor interposed; "I have seen his photograph."

"What does he look like, Irene?" they chorussed. "Men

are no judges."

"He is tall, and dark, and broad-shouldered," Miss Trevor enumerated, as though counting her stitches, "and he has a very firm chin, and a straight nose, and - "

"Perfect!" they cried. "I had an idea he was just like that. I should go wild about him. Does he talk as well as he writes, Mr. Allen?"

"That is admitting that he writes well."

"Admitting?" they shouted scornfully, "and don't you admit it?"

"Some people like his writing, I have to confess," said the Celebrity, with becoming calmness; "certainly his personality could not sell an edition of thirty thousand in a month. I think 'The Sybarites' the best of his works."

"Upon my word, Mr. Allen, I am disgusted with you," said the second voice; "I have not found a man yet who would speak a good word for him. But I did not think it of you."

A woman's tongue, like a firearm, is a dangerous weapon, and often strikes where it is least expected. I saw with a wicked delight that the shot had told, for the Celebrity blushed to the roots of his hair, while Miss Trevor dropped three or four stitches.

"I do not see how you can expect men to like 'The Sybarites'," she said, with some heat; "very few men realize or care to realize what a small chance the average woman has. I know marriage isn't a necessary goal, but most women, as well as most men, look forward to it at some time of life, and, as a rule, a woman is forced to take her choice of the two or three men that offer themselves, no matter what they are. I admire a man who takes up the cudgels for women, as he has done."

"Of course we admire him," they cried, as soon as Miss Trevor had stopped for breath.

"And can you expect a man to like a book which admits that women are the more constant?" she went on.

"Why, Irene, you are quite rabid on the subject," said the second voice; "I did not say I expected it. I only said I had hoped to find Mr. Allen, at least, broad enough to agree with the book."

"Doesn't Mr. Allen remind you a little of Desmond?" asked the first voice, evidently anxious to avoid trouble.

"Do you know whom he took for Desmond, Mr. Allen? I have an idea it was himself."

Mr. Allen, had now recovered some of his composure.

"If so, it was done unconsciously," he said. "I suppose an author must put his best thoughts in the mouth of his hero."

"But it is like him?" she insisted.

"Yes, he holds the same views."

"Which you do not agree with."

"I have not said I did not agree with them," he replied, taking up his own defence; "the point is not that men are more inconstant than women, but that women have more excuse for inconstancy. If I remember correctly, Desmond, in a letter to Rosamond, says: 'Inconstancy in a woman, because of the present social conditions, is often pardonable. In a man, nothing is more despicable.' I think that is so. I believe that a man should stick by the woman to whom he has given his word as closely as he sticks by his friends."

"Ah!" exclaimed the aggressive second voice, "that is all very well. But how about the woman to whom he has not given his word? Unfortunately, the present social conditions allow a man to go pretty far without a definite statement."

At this I could not refrain from looking at Miss Trevor. She was bending over her knitting and had broken her thread.

"It is presumption for a man to speak without some foundation," said the Celebrity, "and wrong unless he is sure of himself."

"But you must admit," the second voice continued, "that a man has no right to amuse himself with a woman, and give her every reason to believe he is going to marry her save the only manly and substantial one. And yet that is something which happens every day. What do you think of a man who deserts a woman under those conditions?"

"He is a detestable dog, of course," declared

the Celebrity.

And the cock in the inn yard was silent.

"I should love to be able to quote from a book at will," said the quieting voice, for the sake of putting an end to an argument which bid fair to become disagreeable. "How do you manage to do it?"

"It was simply a passage that stuck in my mind," he answered modestly; "when I read a book I pick them up just as a roller picks up a sod here and there as it moves over the lawn."

"I should think you might write, Mr. Allen, you have such an original way of putting things!"

"I have thought of it," returned the Celebrity, "and I may, some fine day."

Wherewith he thrust his hands into his pockets and sauntered off with equanimity undisturbed, apparently unaware of the impression he had left behind him. And the Fifth Reader story popped into my head of good King William (or King Frederick, I forgot which), who had a royal fancy for laying aside the gayeties of the court and straying incognito among his plainer subjects, but whose princely origin was invariably detected in spite of any disguise his Majesty could invent.

CHAPTER VII

I experienced a great surprise a few mornings after-wards. I had risen quite early, and found the Celebrity's man superintending the hoisting of luggage on top of a van.

"Is your master leaving?" I asked.

"He's off to Mohair now, sir," said the valet, with a salute.

At that instant the Celebrity himself appeared.

"Yes, old chap, I'm off to Mohair," he explained. "There's more sport in a day up there than you get here in a season. Beastly slow place, this, unless one is a deacon or a doctor of divinity. Why don't you come up, Crocker? Cooke would like nothing better; he has told me so a dozen times."

"He is very good," I replied. I could not resist the temptation to add, "I had an idea Asquith rather suited your purposes just now."

"I don't quite understand," he said, jumping at the other half of my meaning.

"Oh, nothing. But you told me when you came here, if

I am not mistaken, that you chose Asquith because of those very qualities for which you now condemn it."

"Magna est vis consuetudinis," he laughed; "I thought I could stand the life, but I can't. I am tired of their sects and synods and sermons. By the way," said he pulling at my sleeve, "what a deuced pretty girl that Miss Thorn is! Isn't she? Rollins, where's the cart? Well, good-bye, Crocker; see you soon."

He drove rapidly off as the clock struck six, and an uneasy glance he gave the upper windows did not escape me. When Farrar appeared, I told him what had happened.

"Good riddance," he replied sententiously.

We sat in silence until the bell rang, looking at the morning sun on the lake. I was a little anxious to learn the state of Farrar's feelings in regard to Miss Trevor, and how this new twist in affairs had affected them. But I might as well have expected one of King Louis's carp to whisper secrets of the old regime. The young lady came to the breakfast-table looking so fresh and in such high spirits that I made sure she had not heard of the Celebrity's ignoble escape. As the meal proceeded it was easy to mark that her eye now and again fell across his empty chair, and glanced inquiringly towards the door. I made up my mind that I would not be the bearer of evil news, and so did Farrar, so we kept up a vapid small-talk with Mr. Trevor on the condition of trade in the West. Miss Trevor, however, in some way came to suspect that we could account for that vacant seat. At last she fixed her eye inquiringly on me, and I trembled.

"Mr. Crocker," she began, and paused. Then she added with a fair unconcern, "do you happen to know where Mr. Allen is this morning?"

"He has gone over to Mohair, I believe," I replied weakly.

"To Mohair!" she exclaimed, putting down her cup; "why, he promised to go canoeing at ten.

"Probably he will be back by then," I ventured, not finding it in my heart to tell her the cruel truth. But I kept my eyes on my plate. They say a lie has short legs. Mine had, for my black friend, Simpson, was at that instant taking off the fruit, and overheard my remark.

"Mr. Allen done gone for good," he put in, "done give me five dollars last night. Why, sah," he added, scratching his head, "you was on de poch dis mornin' when his trunks was took away!"

It was certainly no time to quibble then.

"His trunks!" Miss Trevor exclaimed.

"Yes, he has left us and gone to Mohair," I said, "bag and baggage. That is the flat truth of it."

I suppose there is some general rule for calculating beforehand how a young woman is going to act when news of this sort is broken. I had no notion of what Miss Trevor would do. I believe Farrar thought she would faint, for he laid his napkin on the table. She did nothing of the kind, but said simply:

"How unreliable men are!"

I fell to guessing what her feelings were; for the life of me I could not tell from her face. I was sorry for Miss Trevor in spite of the fact that she had neglected to ask my advice before falling in love with the Celebrity. I asked her to go canoeing with me. She refused kindly but very firmly.

It is needless to say that the Celebrity did not come back to the inn, and as far as I could see the desertion was designed, cold-blooded, and complete. Miss Trevor remained out of sight during the day of his departure, and at dinner we noticed traces of a storm about her, - a storm which had come and gone. There was an involuntary hush as she entered the dining-room, for Asquith had been buzzing that afternoon over the episode. And I admired the manner in which she bore her inspection. Already rumors of the cause of Mr. Allen's departure were in active circulation, and I was astonished to learn that he had been seen that day seated upon Indian rock with Miss Thorn herself. This piece of news gave me a feeling of insecurity about people, and about women in particular, that I had never before experienced. After holding the Celebrity up to such unmeasured ridicule as she had done, ridicule not without a seasoning of contempt, it was difficult to believe Miss Thorn so inconsistent as to go alone with him to Indian rock; and she was not ignorant of Miss Trevor's experience. But the fact was attested by trustworthy persons.

I have often wondered what prompted me to ask Miss Trevor again to go canoeing. To do myself justice, it was no wish of mine to meddle with or pry into her affairs. Neither did I flatter myself that my poor company would be any consolation for that she had lost. I shall not try to analyze my motive. Suffice it to record that she accepted this second invitation, and I did my best to amuse her by relating a few of my experiences at the bar, and I told that memorable story of Farrar throwing O'Meara into the street. We were getting along famously, when we descried another canoe passing us at some distance, and we both recognized the Celebrity at the paddle by the flannel jacket of his college boat club. And Miss Thorn sat in the bow!

"Do you know anything about that man, Miss Trevor?" I asked abruptly.

She grew scarlet, but replied:

"I know that he is a fraud."

"Anything else?"

"I can't say that I do; that is, nothing but what he has told me."

"If you will forgive my curiosity," I said, "what has he told you?"

"He says he is the author of The Sybarites," she answered, her lip curling, "but of course I do not believe that, now."

"But that happens to be true," I said, smiling.

She clapped her hands.

"I promised him I wouldn't tell," she cried, "but the

minute I get back to the inn I shall publish it."

"No, don't do that just yet," said I.

"Why not? Of course I shall."

I had no definite reason, only a vague hope that we should get some better sort of enjoyment out of the disclosure before the summer was over.

"You see," I said, "he is always getting into scrapes; he is that kind of a man. And it is my humble opinion that he has put his head into a noose this time, for sure. Mr. Allen, of the 'Miles Standish Bicycle Company,' whose name he has borrowed for the occasion, is enough like him in appearance to be his twin brother."

"He has borrowed another man's name!" she exclaimed; "why, that's stealing!"

"No, merely kleptomania," I replied; "he wouldn't be the other man if he could. But it has struck me that the real Mr. Allen might turn up here, or some friend of his, and stir things a bit. My advice to you is to keep quiet, and we may have a comedy worth seeing."

"Well," she remarked, after she had got over a little of her astonishment, "it would be great fun to tell, but I won't if you say so."

I came to, have a real liking for Miss Trevor. Farrar used to smile when I spoke of this, and I never could induce him to go out with us in the canoe, which we did frequently, - in fact, every day I was at Asquith, except of course Sundays. And we grew to understand each other very well. She looked upon me in the same light as did my other friends, - that of a counsellor-at-law, - and I fell unconsciously into the role of her adviser, in which capacity I was the recipient of many confidences I would have got in no other way. That is, in no other way save one, and in that I had no desire to go, even had it been possible. Miss Trevor was only nineteen, and in her eyes I was at least sixty.

"See here, Miss Trevor," I said to her one day after we had become more or less intimate, "of course it's none of my business, but you didn't feel very badly after the Celebrity went away, did you?"

Her reply was frank and rather staggering.

"Yes, I did. I was engaged to him, you know."

"Engaged to him! I had no idea he ever got that far," I exclaimed.

Miss Trevor laughed merrily.

"It was my fault," she said; "I pinned him down, and he had to propose. There was no way out of it. I don't mind telling you."

I did not know whether to be flattered or aggrieved by this avowal.

"You know," she went on, her tone half apologetic, "the day after he came he told me who he was, and I wanted to stop the people we passed and inform them of the lion I was walking with. And I was quite carried away by the honor of his attentions: any girl would have been, you know."

"I suppose so," I assented.

"And I had heard and read so much of him, and I doted on his stories, and all that. His heroes are divine, you must admit. And, Mr. Crocker," she concluded with a charming naivety, "I just made up my mind I would have him."

"Woman proposes, and man disposes," I laughed. "He escaped in spite of you."

She looked at me queerly.

"Only a jest," I said hurriedly; "your escape is the one to be thankful for. You might have married him, like the young woman in The Sybarites. You remember, do you not, that the hero of that book sacrifices himself for the lady who adores him, but whom he has ceased to adore?"

"Yes, I remember," she laughed; "I believe I know that book by heart."

"Think of the countless girls he must have relieved of their affections before their eyes were opened," I continued with mock gravity. "Think of the charred trail he has left behind him. A man of that sort ought to be put under heavy bonds not to break any more hearts. But a kleptomaniac isn't responsible, you understand. And it isn't worth while to bear any malice."

"Oh, I don't bear any malice now," she said. "I did at first, naturally. But it all seems very ridiculous now I have had time to think it over. I believe, Mr. Crocker, that I never really cared for him."

"Simply an idol shattered this time," I suggested, "and not a heart broken."

"Yes, that's it," said she.

"I am glad to hear it," said I, much pleased that she had taken such a sensible view. "But you are engaged to him."

"I was."

"You have broken the engagement, then?"

"No, I - haven't," she said.

"Then he has broken it?"

She did not appear to resent this catechism.

"That's the strange part of it," said Miss Trevor, "he hasn't even thought it necessary."

"It is clear, then, that you are still engaged to him," said I, smiling at her blank face.

"I suppose I am," she cried. "Isn't it awful? What shall I do, Mr. Crocker? You are so sensible, and have had so much experience."

"I beg your pardon," I remarked grimly.

"Oh, you know what I mean: not that kind of experience, of course. But breach of promise cases and that sort of thing. I have a photograph of him with something written over it."

"Something compromising?" I inquired.

"Yes, you would probably call it so," she answered, reddening. "But there is no need of my repeating it. And then I have a lot of other things. If I write to break off the engagement I shall lose dignity, and it will appear as though I had regrets. I don't wish him to think that, of all things. What shall I do?"

"Do nothing," I said.

"What do you mean?"

"Just that. Do not break the engagement, and keep the photograph and other articles for evidence. If he makes any overtures, don't consider them for an instant. And I think, Miss Trevor, you will succeed sooner or later in making him very uncomfortable. Were he any one else I shouldn't advise such a course, but you won't lose any dignity and self-respect by it, as no one will be likely to hear of it. He can't be taken seriously, and plainly he has never taken any one else so. He hasn't even gone to the trouble to notify you that he does not intend marrying you."

I saw from her expression that my suggestion was favorably entertained.

"What a joke it would be!" she cried delightedly.

"And a decided act of charity," I added, "to the next young woman on his list."

CHAPTER VIII

The humor of my proposition appealed more strongly to Miss Trevor than I had looked for, and from that time forward she became her old self again; for, even after she had conquered her love for the Celebrity, the mortification of having been jilted by him remained. Now she had come to look upon the matter in its true proportions, and her anticipation of a possible chance of teaching him a lesson was a pleasure to behold. Our table in the dining-room became again the abode of scintillating wit and caustic repartee, Farrar bracing up to his old standard, and the demand for seats in the vicinity rose to an animated competition. Mr. Charles Wrexell Allen's chair was finally awarded to a nephew of Judge Short, who could turn a story to perfection.

So life at the inn settled down again to what it had been before the Celebrity came to disturb it.

I had my own reasons for staying away from Mohair. More than once as I drove over to the county-seat in my buggy I had met the Celebrity on a tall tandem cart, with one of Mr. Cooke's high-steppers in the lead, and Miss Thorn in the low seat. I had forgotten to mention that my friend was something of a whip. At such times I would bow very civilly and pass on; not without a twinge, I confess. And as the result of one of these meetings I had to retrace several miles of my road for a brief I had forgotten. After that I took another road, several miles longer, for the sight of Miss Thorn with him seriously disturbed my peace of mind. But at length the day came, as I had feared, when circumstances forced me to go to my client's place. One morning Miss Trevor and I were about stepping into the canoe for our customary excursion when one of Mr. Cooke's footmen arrived with a note for each of us. They were from Mrs. Cooke, and requested the pleasure of our company that day for luncheon. "If you were I, would you go?" Miss Trevor asked doubtfully.

"Of course," I replied.

"But the consequences may be unpleasant."

"Don't let them," I said. "Of what use is tact to a woman if not for just such occasions?"

My invitation had this characteristic note tacked on the end of it

"DEAR CROCKER: Where are you? Where is the judge? F. F. C."

I corralled the judge, and we started off across the fields, in no very mild state of fear of that gentleman's wife, whose vigilance was seldom relaxed. And thus we came by a circuitous route to Mohair, the judge occupied by his own guilty thoughts, and I by others not less disturbing. My client welcomed the judge with that warmth of manner which grappled so many of his friends to his heart, and they disappeared together into the Ethiopian card-room, which was filled with the assegais and exclamation point shields Mr. Cooke had had made at the Sawmill at Beaverton.

I learned from one of the lords-in-waiting loafing about the hall that Mrs. Cooke was out on the golf links, chaperoning some of the Asquith young women whose mothers had not seen fit to ostracize Mohair. Mr. Cooke's ten friends were with them. But this discreet and dignified servant could not reveal the whereabouts of Miss Thorn and of Mr. Allen, both of whom I was decidedly anxious to avoid. I was much disgusted, therefore, to come upon the Celebrity in the smoking-room, writing rapidly, with, sheets of manuscript piled beside him. And he was quite good-natured over my intrusion.

"No," said he, "don't go. It's only a short story I promised for a Christmas number. They offered me fifteen cents a word and promised to put my name on the cover in red, so I couldn't very well refuse. It's no inspiration, though, I tell you that." He rose and pressed a bell behind him and ordered whiskeys and ginger ales, as if he were in a hotel." Sit down, Crocker," he said, waving me to a morocco chair. "Why don't you come over to see us oftener?"

"I've been quite busy," I said.

This remark seemed to please him immensely.

"What a sly old chap you are," said he; "really, I shall have to go back to the inn and watch you."

"What the deuce do you mean?" I demanded.

He looked me over in well-bred astonishment and replied:

"Hang me, Crocker, if I can make you out. You seem

to know the world pretty well, and yet when a fellow twits you on a little flirtation you act as though you were going to black his eyes."

"A little flirtation!" I repeated, aghast.

"Oh, well," he said, smiling, "we won't quarrel over a definition. Call it anything you like."

"Don't you think this a little uncalled for?" I asked, beginning to lose my temper.

"Bless you, no. Not among friends: not among such friends as we are."

"I didn't know we were such devilish good friends," I retorted warmly.

"Oh, yes, we are, devilish good friends," he answered with assurance; "known each other from boyhood, and all that. And I say, old chap," he added, "you needn't be jealous of me, you know. I got out of that long ago. And I'm after something else now."

For a space I was speechless. Then the ludicrous side of the matter struck me, and I laughed in spite of myself. Better, after all, to deal with a fool according to his folly. The Celebrity glanced at the door and drew his chair closer to mine.

"Crocker," he said confidentially, "I'm glad you came here to-day. There is a thing or two I wished to consult you about."

"Professional?" I asked, trying to head him off.

"No," he replied, "amateur, - beastly amateur. A bungle, if I ever made one. The truth is, I executed rather a faux pas over there at Asquith. Tell me," said he, diving desperately at the root of it, "how does Miss Trevor feel about my getting out? I meant to let her down easier; 'pon my word, I did."

This is a way rascals have of judging other men by themselves.

"Well;" said I, "it was rather a blow, of course."

"Of course," he assented.

"And all the more unexpected," I went on, "from a man who has written reams on constancy."

I flatter myself that this nearly struck home, for he was plainly annoyed.

"Oh, bother that!" said he. "How many gowns believe in their own sermons? How many lawyers believe in their own arguments?"

"Unhappily, not as many as might."

"I don't object to telling you, old chap," he continued, "that I went in a little deeper than I intended. A good deal deeper, in fact. Miss Trevor is a deuced fine girl, and all that; but absolutely impossible. I forgot myself, and I confess I was pretty close to caught."

"I congratulate you," I said gravely.

"That's the point of it. I don't know that I'm out of the woods yet. I wanted to see you and find out how she was acting."

My first impulse was to keep him in hot water. Fortunately I thought twice.

"I don't know anything about Miss Trevor's feelings - " I began.

"Naturally not - " he interrupted, with a smile.

"But I have a notion that, if she ever fancied you, she doesn't care a straw for you to-day."

"Doesn't she now," he replied somewhat regretfully. Here was one of the knots in his character I never could untie.

"Understand, that is simply my guess," I said. "You must have discovered that it is never possible to be sure of a woman's feelings."

"Found that out long ago," he replied with conviction, and added: "Then you think I need not anticipate any trouble from her?"

"I have told you what I think," I answered; "you know better than I what the situation is."

He still lingered.

"Does she appear to be in, - ah, - in good spirits?"

I had work to keep my face straight.

"Capital," I said; "I never saw her happier."

This seemed to satisfy him.

"Downcast at first, happy now," he remarked thoughtfully. "Yes, she got over it. I'm much obliged to you, Crocker."

I left him to finish his short story and walked out across the circle of smooth lawn towards the golf links. And there I met Mrs. Cooke and her niece coming in together. The warm red of her costume became Miss Thorn wonderfully, and set off the glossy black of her hair. And her skin was glowing from the exercise. An involuntary feeling of admiration for this tall, athletic young woman swept over me, and I halted in my steps for no other reason, I believe, than that I might look upon her the longer.

What man, I thought resentfully, would not travel a thousand miles to be near her?

"It is Mr. Crocker," said Mrs. Cooke; "I had given up all hope of ever seeing you again. Why have you been such a stranger?"

"As if you didn't know, Aunt Maria," Miss Thorn put in gayly.

"Oh yes, I know," returned her aunt, "and I have not been foolish enough to invite the bar without the magnet. And yet, Mr. Crocker," she went on playfully, "I had imagined that you were the one man in a hundred who did not need an inducement."

Miss Thorn began digging up the turf with her lofter: it was a painful moment for me.

"You might at least have tried me, Mrs. Cooke," I said.

Miss Thorn looked up quickly from the ground, her eyes searchingly upon my face. And Mrs. Cooke seemed surprised.

"We are glad you came, at any rate," she answered.

And at luncheon my seat was next to Miss Thorn's, while the Celebrity was placed at the right of Miss Trevor. I observed that his face went blank from time to time at some quip of hers: even a dull woman may be sharp under such circumstances, and Miss Trevor had wits to spare. And I marked that she never allowed her talk with him to drift into deep water; when there was danger of this she would draw the entire table into their conversation by some adroit remark, or create a laugh at his expense. As for me, I held a discreet if uncomfortable silence, save for the few words which passed between Miss Thorn and me. Once or twice I caught her covert glance on me. But I felt, and strongly, that there could be no friendship between us now, and I did not care to dissimulate merely for the sake of appearances. Besides, I was not a little put out over the senseless piece of gossip which had gone abroad concerning me.

It had been arranged as part of the day's programme that Mr. Cooke was to drive those who wished to go over the Rise in his new brake. But the table was not graced by our host's presence, Mrs. Cooke apologizing for him, explaining that he had disappeared quite mysteriously. It turned out that he and the judge had been served with luncheon in the Ethiopian card-room, and neither threats nor fair words could draw him away. The judge had not held such cards for years, and it was in vain that I talked to him of consequences. The Ten decided to remain and watch a game which was pronounced little short of phenomenal, and my client gave orders for the smaller brake and requested the Celebrity to drive. And this he was nothing loth to do. For the edification as well as the assurance of the party Mr. Allen explained, while we were waiting under the porte cochere, how he had driven the Windsor coach down Piccadilly at the height of the season, with a certain member of Parliament and noted whip on the box seat.

And, to do him justice, he could drive. He won the instant respect of Mr. Cooke's coachman by his manner of taking up the lines, and clinched it when he dropped a careless remark concerning the off wheeler. And after the critical inspection of the horses which is proper he climbed up on the box. There was much hesitation among the ladies as to who should take the seat of honor: Mrs. Cooke declining, it was pressed upon Miss Thorn. But she, somewhat to my surprise, declined also, and it was finally filled by a young woman from Asquith.

As we drove off I found myself alone with Mrs. Cooke's niece on the seat behind.

The day was cool and snappy for August, and the Rise all green with a lavish nature. Now we, plunged into a deep shade with the boughs lacing each other overhead, and crossed dainty, rustic bridges over the cold trout-streams, the boards giving back the clatter of our horses' feet: or anon we shot into a clearing, with a colored glimpse of the lake and its curving shore far below us. I had always loved that piece of country since the first look I had of it from the Asquith road, and the sight of it rarely failed to set my blood a-tingle with pleasure. But to-day I scarcely saw it. I wondered what whim had impelled Miss Thorn to get into this seat. She paid but little attention to me during the first part of the drive, though a mere look in my direction seemed to afford her amusement. And at last, half way up the Rise, where the road takes to an embankment, I got a decided jar.

"Mr. Allen," she cried to the Celebrity, "you must stop here. Do you remember how long we tarried over this bit on Friday?"

He tightened the lines and threw a meaning glance backward.

I was tempted to say:

"You and Mr. Allen should know these roads rather well, Miss Thorn."

"Every inch of them," she replied.

We must have gone a mile farther when she turned upon me.

"It is your duty to be entertaining, Mr. Crocker. What in the world are you thinking of, with your brow all puckered up, forbidding as an owl?"

"I was thinking how some people change," I answered, with a readiness which surprised me.

"Strange," she said, "I had the same thing in mind. I hear decidedly queer tales of you; canoeing every day that business does not prevent, and whole evenings spent at the dark end of a veranda."

"What rubbish!" I exclaimed, not knowing whether to be angered or amused.

"Come, sir," she said, with mock sternness, "answer the charge. Guilty or not guilty?"

"First let me make a counter-charge," said I; "you have given me the right. Not long ago a certain young lady came to Mohair and found there a young author of note with whom she had had some previous acquaintance. She did not hesitate to intimate her views on the character of this Celebrity, and her views were not favorable."

I paused. There was some satisfaction in seeing Miss Thorn biting her lip.

"Well?"

"Not at all favorable, mind you," I went on. "And the young lady's general appearance was such as to lead one to suppose her the sincerest of persons. Now I am at a loss to account for a discrepancy between her words and her actions."

While I talked Miss Thorn's face had been gradually turning from mine until now I saw only the dainty knot at the back of her head. Her shoulders were quivering with laughter. But presently her face came back all gravity, save a suspicious gleam of mirth in the eyes.

"It does seem inconsistent, Mr. Crocker; I grant you that. No doubt it is so. But let me ask you something:

did you ever yet know a woman who was not inconsistent?"

I did not realize I had been side-tracked until I came to think over this conversation afterwards.

"I am not sure," I replied. "Perhaps I merely hoped that one such existed."

She dropped her eyes.

"Then don't be surprised at my failing," said she. "No doubt I criticised the Celebrity severely. I cannot recall what I said. But it is upon the better side of a character that we must learn to look. Did it ever strike you that the Celebrity had some exceedingly fine qualities?"

"No, it did not," I answered positively.

"Nevertheless, he has," she went on, in all apparent seriousness. "He drives almost as well as Uncle Farquhar, dances well, and is a capital paddle."

"You were speaking of qualities, not accomplishments," I said. A horrible suspicion that she was having a little fun at my expense crossed my mind.

Very good, then. You must admit that he is generous to a fault, amiable; and persevering, else he would never have attained the position he enjoys. And his affection for you, Mr. Crocker, is really touching, considering how little he gets in return."

"Come, Miss Thorn," I said severely, "this is ridiculous. I don't like him, and never shall. I liked him once, before he took to writing drivel. But he must have been made over since then. And what is more, with all respect to your opinion, I don't believe he likes me."

Miss Thorn straightened up with dignity and said:

"You do him an injustice. But perhaps you will learn to appreciate him before he leaves Mohair."

"That is not likely," I replied - not at all pleasantly, I fear. And again I thought I observed in her the same desire to laugh she had before exhibited.

And all the way back her talk was of nothing except the Celebrity. I tried every method short of absolute rudeness to change the subject, and went from silence to taciturnity and back again to silence. She discussed his books and his mannerisms, even the growth of his popularity. She repeated anecdotes of him from Naples to St. Petersburg, from Tokio to Cape Town. And when we finally stopped under the porte cochere I had scarcely the civility left to say good-bye.

I held out my hand to help her to the ground, but she paused on the second step.

"Mr. Crocker," she observed archly, "I believe you once told me you had not known many girls in your life."

"True," I said; "why do you ask?"

"I wished to be sure of it," she replied.

And jumping down without my assistance, she laughed and disappeared into the house.

VOLUME 3.

CHAPTER IX

That evening I lighted a cigar and went down to sit on the outermost pile of the Asquith dock to commune with myself. To say that I was disappointed in Miss Thorn would be to set a mild value on my feelings. I was angry, even aggressive, over her defence of the Celebrity. I had gone over to Mohair that day with a hope that some good reason was at the bottom of her tolerance for him, and had come back without any hope. She not only tolerated him, but, wonderful to be said, plainly liked him. Had she not praised him, and defended him, and become indignant when I spoke my mind about him? And I would have taken my oath, two weeks before, that nothing short of hypnotic influence could have changed her. By her own confession she had come to Asquith with her eyes opened, and, what was more, seen another girl wrecked on the same reef.

Farrar followed me out presently, and I had an impulse to submit the problem as it stood to him. But it was a long story, and I did not believe that if he were in my boots he would have consulted me. Again, I sometimes thought Farrar yearned for confidences, though it was impossible for him to confide. And he wore an inviting air to-night. Then, as everybody knows, there is that about twilight and an after-dinner cigar which leads to communication. They are excellent solvents. My friend seated himself on the pile next to mine, and said,

"It strikes me you have been behaving rather queer lately, Crocker."

This was clearly an invitation from Farrar, and I melted.

"I admit," said I, "that I am a good deal perplexed over the contradictions of the human mind."

"Oh, is that all?" he replied dryly. "I supposed it was worse. Narrower, I mean. Didn't know you ever bothered yourself with abstract philosophy."

"See here, Farrar," said I, "what is your opinion of Miss Thorn?"

He stopped kicking his feet against the pile and looked up.

"Miss Thorn?"

"Yes, Miss Thorn," I repeated with emphasis. I knew he had in mind that abominable twaddle about the canoe excursions.

"Why, to tell the truth," said he, "I never had any opinion of Miss Thorn."

"You mean you never formed any, I suppose," I returned with some tartness.

"Yes, that is it. How darned precise you are getting, Crocker! One would think you were going to write a rhetoric. What put Miss Thorn into your head?"

"I have been coaching beside her this afternoon."

"Oh!" said Farrar.

"Do you remember the night she came," I asked, "and we sat with her on the Florentine porch, and Charles Wrexell recognized her and came up?"

"Yes," he replied with awakened interest, "and I meant to ask you about that."

"Miss Thorn had met him in the East. And I gathered from what she told me that he has followed her out here."

"Shouldn't wonder," said Farrar. "Don't much blame him, do you? Is that what troubles you?" he asked, in surprise.

"Not precisely," I answered vaguely; "but from what she has said then and since, she made it pretty clear that she hadn't any use for him; saw through him, you know."

"Pity her if she didn't. But what did she say?"

I repeated the conversations I had had with Miss Thorn, without revealing Mr. Allen's identity with the celebrated author.

"That is rather severe," he assented.

"He decamped for Mohair, as you know, and since that time she has gone back on every word of it. She is with him morning and evening, and, to crown all, stood up for him through thick and thin to-day, and praised him. What do you think of that?"

"What I should have expected in a woman," said he, nonchalantly.

"They aren't all alike," I retorted.

He shook out his pipe, and getting down from his high seat laid his hand on my knee.

"I thought so once, old fellow," he whispered, and went off down the dock.

This was the nearest Farrar ever came to a confidence.

I have now to chronicle a curious friendship which had its beginning at this time. The friendships of the other sex are quickly made, and sometimes as quickly dissolved. This one interested me more than I care to own. The next morning Judge Short, looking somewhat dejected after the overnight conference he had had with his wife, was innocently and somewhat ostentatiously engaged in tossing quoits with me in front of the inn, when Miss Thorn drove up in a basket cart. She gave me a bow which proved that she bore no ill-will for that which I had said about her hero. Then Miss Trevor appeared, and away they went together. This was the commencement. Soon the acquaintance became an intimacy, and their lives a series of visits to each other. Although this new state of affairs did not seem to decrease the number of Miss Thorn's 'tete-a-tetes' with the Celebrity, it put a stop to the canoe expeditions I had been in the habit of taking with Miss Trevor, which I thought just as well under the circumstances. More than once Miss Thorn partook of the inn fare at our table, and when this happened I would make my escape before the coffee. For such was the nature of my feelings regarding the Celebrity that I could not bring myself into cordial relations with one who professed to admire him. I realize how ridiculous such a sentiment must appear, but it existed nevertheless, and most strongly.

I tried hard to throw Miss Thorn out of my thoughts, and very nearly succeeded. I took to spending more and more of my time at the county- seat, where I remained for days at a stretch, inventing business when there was none. And in the meanwhile I lost all respect for myself as a sensible man, and cursed the day the Celebrity came into the state. It seemed strange that this acquaintance of my early days should have come back into my life, transformed, to make it more or less miserable. The county-seat being several miles inland, and lying in the midst of hills, could get intolerably hot in September. At last I was driven out in spite of myself, and I arrived at Asquith cross and dusty. As Simpson was brushing me off, Miss Trevor came up the path looking cool and pretty in a summer gown, and her face expressed sympathy. I have never denied that sympathy was a good thing.

"Oh, Mr. Crocker," she cried, "I am so glad you are back again! We have missed you dreadfully. And you look tired, poor man, quite worn out. It is a shame you have to go over to that hot place to work."

I agreed with her.

"And I never have any one to take me canoeing any more."

"Let's go now," I suggested, "before dinner."

So we went. It was a keen pleasure to be on the lake again after the sultry court-rooms and offices, and the wind and exercise quickly brought back my appetite and spirits. I paddled hither and thither, stopping now and then to lie under the pines at the mouth of some stream, while Miss Trevor talked. She was almost a child in her eagerness to amuse me with the happenings since my departure. This was always her manner with me, in curious contrast to her habit of fencing and playing with words when in company. Presently she burst out:

"Mr. Crocker, why is it that you avoid Miss Thorn? I was talking of you to her only to-day, and she says you go miles out of your way to get out of speaking to her; that you seemed to like her quite well at first. She couldn't understand the change."

"Did she say that?" I exclaimed.

"Indeed, she did; and I have noticed it, too. I saw you leave before coffee more than once when she was here. I don't believe you know what a fine girl she is."

"Why, then, does she accept and return the attentions of the Celebrity?" I inquired, with a touch of acidity. "She knows what he is as well, if not better, than you or I. I own I can't understand it," I said, the subject getting ahead of me. "I believe she is in love with him."

Miss Trevor began to laugh; quietly at first, and, as her merriment increased, heartily.

"Shouldn't we be getting back?" I asked, looking at my watch. "It lacks but half an hour of dinner."

"Please don't be angry, Mr. Crocker," she pleaded. "I really couldn't help laughing."

"I was unaware I had said anything funny, Miss Trevor," I replied.

"Of course you didn't," she said more soberly; "that is, you didn't intend to. But the very notion of Miss Thorn in love with the Celebrity is funny."

"Evidence is stronger than argument," said I. "And now she has even convicted herself."

I started to paddle homeward, rather furiously, and my companion said nothing until we came in sight of the inn. As the canoe glided into the smooth surface behind the breakwater, she broke the silence.

"I heard you went fishing the other day," said she.

"Yes."

"And the judge told me about a big bass you hooked, and how you played him longer than was necessary for the mere fun of the thing."

"Yes."

"Perhaps you will find in the feeling that prompted you to do that a clue to the character of our sex."

CHAPTER X

Mr. Cooke had had a sloop yacht built at Far Harbor, the completion of which had been delayed, and which was but just delivered. She was, painted white, with brass fittings, and under her stern, in big, black letters, was the word Maria, intended as a surprise and delicate conjugal compliment to Mrs. Cooke. The Maria had a cabin, which was finished in hard wood and yellow plush, and accommodations for keeping things cold. This last Mr. Cooke had insisted upon.

The skipper Mr. Cooke had hired at Far Harbor was a God-fearing man with a luke warm interest in his new billet and employer, and had only been prevailed upon to take charge of the yacht for the month after the offer of an emolument equal to half a year's sea pay of an ensign in the navy. His son and helper was to receive a sum proportionally exorbitant. This worthy man sighted Mohair on a Sunday morning, and at nine o'clock dropped his anchor with a salute which caused Mr. Cooke to say unpleasant things in his sleep. After making things ship-shape and hoisting the jack, both father and son rowed ashore to the little church at Asquith.

Now the butler at Mohair was a servant who had learned, from long experience, to anticipate every wish and whim of his master, and from the moment he descried the white sails of the yacht out of the windows of the butler's pantry his duty was clear as daylight. Such was the comprehension and despatch with which he gave his commands that the captain returned from divine worship to find the Maria in profane hands, her immaculate deck littered with straw and sawdust, and covered to the coamings with bottles and cases. This decided the captain, he packed his kit in high dudgeon, and took the first train back to Far Harbor, leaving the yacht to her fate.

This sudden and inconsiderate departure was a severe blow to Mr. Cooke' who was so constituted that he cared but little about anything until there was danger of not getting it. My client had planned a trip to Bear Island for the following Tuesday, which was to last a week, the party to bring tents with them and rough it, with the Maria as headquarters. It was out of the question to send to Far Harbor for another skipper, if, indeed, one could be found at that late period. And as luck would have it, six of Mr. Cooke's ten guests had left but a day or so since, and among them had been the only yacht-owner. None of the four that remained could do more than haul aft and belay a sheet. But the Celebrity, who chanced along as Mr. Cooke was ruefully gazing at the graceful lines of the Maria from the wharf and cursing the fate that kept him ashore with a stiff wind blowing, proposed a way out of the difficulty. He, the Celebrity, would gladly sail the Maria over to Bear Island provided another man could be found to relieve him occasionally at the wheel, and the like. He had noticed that Farrar was a capable hand in a boat, and suggested that he be sent for.

This suggestion Mr. Cooke thought so well of that he hurried over to Asquith to consult Farrar at once, and incidentally to consult me. We can hardly be blamed for receiving his overtures with a moderate enthusiasm. In fact, we were of one mind not to go when the subject was first broached. But my client had a persuasive way about him that was irresistible, and the mere mention of the favors he had conferred upon both of us at different periods of our lives was sufficient. We consented.

Thus it came to pass that Tuesday morning found the party assembled on the wharf at Mohair, the Four and the Celebrity, as well as Mr. Cooke, having produced yachting suits from their inexhaustible wardrobes. Mr. Trevor and his daughter, Mrs. Cooke and Miss Thorn, and Farrar and myself completed the party. We were to adhere strictly to primeval principles: the ladies were not permitted a maid, while the Celebrity was forced to leave his manservant, and Mr. Cooke his chef. I had, however, thrust into my pocket the Minneapolis papers, which had been handed me by the clerk on their arrival at the inn, which happened just as I was leaving. 'Quod bene notandum!'

Thereby hangs a tale!

For the northern lakes the day was rather dead: a little wind lay in the southeast, scarcely enough to break the water, with the sky an intense blue. But the Maria was hardly cast and under way before it became painfully apparent that the Celebrity was much better fitted to lead a cotillon than to sail a boat. He gave his orders, nevertheless, in a firm, seamanlike fashion, though with no great pertinence, and thus managed to establish the confidence of Mr. Cooke. Farrar, after setting things to rights, joined Mrs. Cooke and me over the cabin.

"How about hoisting the spinnaker, mate?" the Celebrity shouted after him.

Farrar did not deign to answer: his eye was on the wind. And the boom, which had been acting uneasily, finally decided to gybe, and swept majestically over, carrying two of the Four in front of it, and all but dropped them into the water.

"A common occurrence in a light breeze," we heard the Celebrity reassure Mr. Cooke and Miss Thorn.

"The Maria has vindicated her sex," remarked Farrar.

We laughed.

"Why don't you sail, Mr. Farrar?" asked Mrs. Cooke.

"He can't do any harm in this breeze," Farrar replied; "it isn't strong enough to get anywhere with."

He was right. The boom gybed twenty times that morning, and the Celebrity offered an equal number of apologies. Mr. Cooke and the Four vanished, and from the uproarious laughter which arose from the cabin transoms I judged they were telling stories. While Miss Thorn spent the time profitably in learning how to conn a yacht. At one, when we had luncheon, Mohair was still in the distance. At two it began to cloud over, the wind fell flat, and an ominous black bank came up from the south. Without more ado, Farrar, calling on me to give him a hand, eased down the halliards and began to close reef the mainsail.

"Hold on," said the Celebrity, "who told you to do that?"

"I am very sure you didn't," Farrar returned, as he hauled out a reef earing.

Here a few drops of rain on the deck warned the ladies to retire to the cabin.

"Take the helm until I get my mackintosh, will you, Farrar?" said the Celebrity, "and be careful what you do."

Farrar took the helm and hauled in the sheet, while the Celebrity, Mr. Cooke, and the guests donned their rain-clothes. The water ahead was now like blue velvet, and the rain pelting. The Maria was heeling to the squall by the time the Celebrity appeared at the cabin door, enveloped in an ample waterproof, a rubber cover on his yachting cap. A fool despises a danger he has never experienced, and our author, with a remark about a spanking breeze, made a motion to take the wheel. But Farrar, the flannel of his shirt clinging to the muscular outline of his shoulders, gave him a push which sent him sprawling against the lee refrigerator. Well Miss Thorn was not there to see.

"You will have to answer for this," he cried, as he scrambled to his feet and clutched the weather wash-board with one hand, while he shook the other in Farrar's face.

"Crocker," said Farrar to me, coolly, "keep that idiot out of the way for a while, or we'll all be drowned. Tie him up, if necessary."

I was relieved from this somewhat unpleasant task. Mr. Cooke, with his back to the rain, sat an amused witness to the mutiny, as blissfully ignorant as the Celebrity of the character of a lake squall.

"I appeal to you, as the owner of this yacht, Mr. Cooke," the Celebrity shouted, "whether, as the person delegated by you to take charge of it, I am to suffer indignity and insult. I have sailed larger yachts than this time and again on the coast, at - " here he swallowed a portion of a wave and was mercifully prevented from being specific.

But Mr. Cooke was looking a trifle bewildered. It was hardly possible for him to cling to the refrigerator, much less quell a mutiny. One who has sailed the lakes well knows how rapidly they can be lashed to fury by a storm, and the wind was now spinning the tops of the waves into a blinding spray. Although the Maria proved a stiff boat and a seaworthy, she was not altogether without motion; and the set expression on Farrar's face would have told me, had I not known it, that our situation at that moment was no joke. Repeatedly, as she was held up to it, a precocious roller would sweep from bow to stern, until we without coats were wet and shivering.

The close and crowded cabin of a small yacht is not an attractive place in rough weather; and one by one the Four emerged and distributed themselves about the deck, wherever they could obtain a hold. Some of them began to act peculiarly. Upon Mr. Cooke's unwillingness or inability to interfere in his behalf, the Celebrity had assumed an aggrieved demeanor, but soon the motion of the Maria became more and more pronounced, and the difficulty of maintaining his decorum likewise increased. The ruddy color left his face, which grew pale with effort. I will do him the justice to say that the effort was heroic: he whistled popular airs, and snatches of the grand opera; he relieved Mr. Cooke of his glasses (of which Mr. Cooke had neglected to relieve himself), and scanned the sea line busily. But the inevitable deferred is frequently more violent than the inevitable taken gracefully, and the confusion which at length overtook the Celebrity was utter as his humiliation was complete. We laid him beside Mr. Cooke in the cockpit.

The rain presently ceased, and the wind hauled, as is often the case, to the northwest, which began to clear, while Bear Island rose from the northern horizon. Both Farrar and I were surprised to see Miss Trevor come out; she hooked back the cabin doors and surveyed the prostrate forms with amusement.

We asked her about those inside.

"Mrs. Cooke has really been very ill," she said, "and Miss Thorn is doing all she can for her. My father and I were more fortunate. But you will both catch your deaths," she exclaimed, noticing our condition. "Tell me where I can find your coats."

I suppose it is natural for a man to enjoy being looked after in this way; it was certainly a new sensation to Farrar and myself. We assured her we were drying out and did not need the coats, but nevertheless she went back into the cabin and found them.

"Miss Thorn says you should both be whipped," she remarked.

When we had put on our coats Miss Trevor sat down and began to talk.

"I once heard of a man," she began complacently, "a man that was buried alive, and who contrived to dig himself up and then read his own epitaph. It did not please him, but he was wise and amended his life. I have often thought how much it might help some people if they could read their own epitaphs."

Farrar was very quick at this sort of thing; and now that the steering had become easier was only too glad to join her in worrying the Celebrity. But he, if he were conscious, gave no sign of it.

"They ought to be buried so that they could not dig themselves up," he said. "The epitaphs would only strengthen their belief that they had lived in an unappreciative age."

"One I happen to have in mind, however, lives in an appreciative age. Most appreciative."

"And women are often epitaph-makers."

"You are hard on the sex, Mr. Farrar," she answered, "but perhaps justly so. And yet there are some women I know of who would not write an epitaph to his taste."

Farrar looked at her curiously.

"I beg your pardon," he said.

"Do not imagine I am touchy on the subject," she replied quickly; "some of us are fortunate enough to have had our eyes opened."

I thought the Celebrity stirred uneasily.

"Have you read The Sybarites?" she asked.

Farrar was puzzled.

"No," said he sententiously, "and I don't want to."

"I know the average man thinks it a disgrace to have read it. And you may not believe me when I say that it is a strong story of its kind, with a strong moral. There are men who might read that book and be a great deal better for it. And, if they took the moral to heart, it would prove every bit as effectual as their own epitaphs."

He was not quite sure of her drift, but he perceived that she was still making fun of Mr. Allen.

"And the moral?" he inquired.

"Well," she said, "the best I can do is to give you a synopsis of the story, and then you can judge of its fitness. The hero is called Victor Desmond. He is a young man of a sterling though undeveloped character, who has been hampered by an indulgent parent with a large fortune. Desmond is a butterfly, and sips life after the approved manner of his kind, - now from Bohemian glass, now from vessels of gold and silver. He chats with stage lights in their dressing-rooms, and attends a ball in the Bowery or a supper at Sherry's with a ready versatility. The book, apart from its intention, really gives the middle classes an excellent idea of what is called 'high-life.'

"It is some time before Desmond discovers that he possesses the gift of Paris, - a deliberation proving his lack of conceit, - that wherever he goes he unwittingly breaks a heart, and sometimes two or three. This discovery is naturally so painful that he comes home to his chambers and throws himself on a lounge before his fire in a fit of self-deprecation, and reflects on a misspent and foolish life. This, mind you, is where his character starts to develop. And he makes a heroic resolve, not to cut off his nose or to grow a beard, nor get married, but henceforth to live a life of usefulness and seclusion, which was certainly considerate. And furthermore, if by any accident he ever again involved the affections of another girl he would marry her, be she as ugly as sin or as poor as poverty. Then the heroine comes in. Her name is Rosamond, which sounds well and may be euphoniously coupled with Desmond; and, with the single exception of a boarding-school girl, she is the only young woman he ever thought of twice. In order to save her and himself he goes away, but the temptation to write to her overpowers him, and of course she answers his letter. This brings on a correspondence. His letters take the form of confessions, and are the fruits of much philosophical reflection. 'Inconstancy in woman,' he says, because of the present social conditions, is often pardonable. In a man, nothing is more despicable.' This is his cardinal principle, and he sticks to it nobly. For, though he tires of Rosamond, who is quite attractive, however, he marries her and lives a life of self-denial. There are men who might take that story to heart."

I was amused that she should give the passage quoted by the Celebrity himself. Her double meaning was, naturally, lost on Farrar, but he enjoyed the thing hugely, nevertheless, as more or less applicable to Mr. Allen. I made sure that gentleman was sensible of what was being said, though he scarcely moved a muscle. And Miss Trevor, with a mirthful glance at me that was not without a tinge of triumph, jumped lightly to the deck and went in to see the invalids.

We were now working up into the lee of the island, whose tall pines stood clean and black against the red glow of the evening sky. Mr. Cooke began to give evidences of life, and finally got up and overhauled one of the ice-chests for a restorative. Farrar put into the little cove, where we dropped anchor, and soon had the chief sufferers ashore; and a delicate supper, in the preparation of which Miss Thorn showed her ability as a cook, soon restored them. For my part, I much preferred Miss Thorn's dishes to those of the Mohair chef, and so did Farrar. And the Four, surprising as it may seem, made themselves generally useful about the camp in pitching the tents under Farrar's supervision. But the Celebrity remained apart and silent.

CHAPTER XI

Our first, night in the Bear Island camp passed without incident, and we all slept profoundly, tired out by the labors of the day before. After breakfast, the Four set out to explore, with trout-rods and shot-guns. Bear Island is, with the exception of the cove into which we had put, as nearly round as an island can be, and perhaps three miles in diameter. It has two clear brooks which, owing to the comparative inaccessibility of the place, still contain trout and grayling, though there are few spots where a fly can be cast on account of the dense underbrush. The woods contain partridge, or ruffed grouse, and other game in smaller quantities. I believe my client entertained some notion of establishing a preserve here.

The insults which had been heaped upon the Celebrity on the yacht seemed to have raised rather than lowered him in Miss Thorn's esteem, for these two ensconced themselves among the pines above the camp with an edition de luxe of one of his works which she had brought along. They were soon absorbed in one of those famous short stories of his with the ending left open to discussion. Mr. Cooke was indisposed. He had not yet recovered from the shaking up his system had sustained, and he took to a canvas easy chair he had brought with him and placed a decanter of Scotch and a tumbler of ice at his side. The efficacy of this remedy was assured. And he demanded the bunch of news-papers he spied protruding from my pocket.

The rest of us were engaged in various occupations: Mr. Trevor relating experiences of steamboat days on the Ohio to Mrs. Cooke; Miss Trevor buried in a serial in the Century; and Farrar and I taking an inventory of fishing-tackle, when we were startled by aloud and profane ejaculation. Mr. Cooke had hastily put down his glass and was staring at the newspaper before him with eyes as large as after-dinner coffee-cups.

"Come here," he shouted over at us. "Come here, Crocker," he repeated, seeing we were slow to move. "For God's sake, come here!"

In obedience to this emphatic summons I crossed the stream and drew near to Mr. Cooke, who was busily pouring out another glass of whiskey to tide him over this strange excitement. But, as Mr. Cooke was easily excited and on such occasions always drank whiskey to quiet his nerves, I thought nothing of it. He was sitting bolt upright and held out the paper to me with a shaking hand, while he pointed to some headlines on the first page. And this is what I read:

TREASURER TAKES A TRIP.

CHARLES WREXELL ALLEN, OF THE MILES STANDISH BICYCLE COMPANY, GETS OFF WITH 100,000 DOLLARS.

DETECTIVES BAFFLED.

THE ABSCONDER A BACK BAY SOCIAL LEADER.

Half way down the column was a picture of Mr. Allen, a cut made from a photograph, and, allowing for the crudities of newspaper reproduction, it was a striking likeness of the Celebrity. Underneath was a short description. Mr. Allen was five feet eleven (the Celebrity's height), had a straight nose, square chin, dark hair and eyes, broad shoulders, was dressed elaborately; in brief, tallied in every particular with the Celebrity with the exception of the slight scar which Allen was thought to have on his forehead.

The situation and all its ludicrous possibilities came over me with a jump. It was too good to be true. Had Mr. Charles Wrexell Allen arrived at Asquith and created a sensation with the man who stole his name I should have been amply satisfied. But that Mr. Allen had been obliging enough to abscond with a large sum of money was beyond dreaming!

I glanced at the rest of it: a history of the well-established company followed, with all that Mr. Allen had done for it. The picture, by the way, had been obtained from the St. Paul agent of the bicycle. After doing due credit to the treasurer's abilities as a hustler there followed a summary of his character, hitherto without reproach; but his tastes were expensive ones. Mr. Allen's tendency to extravagance had been noticed by the members of the Miles Standish Company, and some of the older directors had on occasions remonstrated with him. But he had been too valuable a man to let go, and it seems as treasurer he was trusted implicitly. He was said to have more clothes than any man in Boston.

I am used to thinking quickly, and by the time I had read this I had an idea.

"What in hell do you make of that, Crocker?" cried my client, eyeing me closely and repeating the question again and again, as was his wont when agitated.

"It is certainly plain enough," I replied, "but I should like to talk to you before you decide to hand him over to the authorities."

I thought I knew Mr. Cooke, and I was not mistaken.

"Authorities!" he roared. "Damn the authorities! There's my yacht, and there's the Canadian border." And he pointed to the north.

The others were pressing around us by this time, and had caught the significant words which Mr. Cooke had uttered. I imagine that if my client had stopped to think twice, which of course is a preposterous condition, he would have confided his discovery only to Farrar and to me. It was now out of the question to keep it from the rest of the party, and Mr. Trevor got the headlines over my shoulder. I handed him the sheet.

"Read it, Mr. Trevor," said Mrs. Cooke.

Mr. Trevor, in a somewhat unsteady voice, read the headlines and began the column, and they followed breathless with astonishment and agitation. Once or twice the senator paused to frown upon the Celebrity with a terrible sternness, thus directing all other eyes to him. His demeanor was a study in itself. It may be surmised, from what I have said of him, that there was a strain of the actor in his composition; and I am prepared to make an affidavit that, secure in the knowledge that he had witnesses present to attest his identity, he hugely enjoyed the sensation he was creating. That he looked forward with a profound pleasure to the stir which the disclosure that he was the author of The Sybarites would make. His face wore a beatific smile.

As Mr. Trevor continued, his voice became firmer and his manner more majestic. It was a task distinctly to his taste, and one might have thought he was reading the sentence of a Hastings. I was standing next to his daughter. The look of astonishment, perhaps of horror, which I had seen on her face when her father first began to read had now faded into something akin to wickedness. Did she wink? I can't say, never before having had a young woman wink at me. But the next moment her vinaigrette was rolling down the bank towards the brook, and I was after it. I heard her close behind me. She must have read my intentions by a kind of mental telepathy.

"Are you going to do it?" she whispered.

"Of course," I answered. "To miss such a chance would be a downright sin."

There was a little awe in her laugh.

"Miss Thorn is the only obstacle," I added, "and Mr. Cooke is our hope. I think he will go by me."

"Don't let Miss Thorn worry you," she said as we climbed back.

"What do you mean?" I demanded. But she only shook her head. We were at the top again, and Mr. Trevor was reading an appended despatch from Buffalo, stating that Mr. Allen had been recognized there, in the latter part of June, walking up and down the platform of the station, in a smoking-jacket, and that he had climbed on the Chicago limited as it pulled out. This may have caused the Celebrity to feel a trifle uncomfortable.

"Ha!" exclaimed Mr. Trevor, as he put down the paper. "Mr. Cooke, do you happen to have any handcuffs on the Maria?"

But my client was pouring out a stiff helping from the decanter, which he still held in his hand. Then he approached the Celebrity.

"Don't let it worry you, old man," said he, with intense earnestness. "Don't let it worry you. You're my guest, and I'll see you safe out of it, or bust."

"Fenelon," said Mrs. Cooke, gravely, "do you realize what you are saying?"

"You're a clever one, Allen," my client continued, and he backed away the better to look him over; "you had nerve to stay as long as you did."

The Celebrity laughed confidently.

"Cooke," he replied, "I appreciate your generosity, - I really do. I know no offence is meant. The mistake is, in fact, most pardonable."

In Mr. Cooke amazement and admiration were clamoring for utterance.

"Damn me," he sputtered, "if you're not the coolest embezzler I ever saw."

The Celebrity laughed again. Then he surveyed the circle.

"My friends," he said, "this is certainly a most amazing coincidence; one which, I assure you, surprises me no less than it does you. You have no doubt remarked that I have my peculiarities. We all have.

"I flatter thyself I am not entirely unknown. And the annoyances imposed upon me by a certain fame I have achieved had become such that some months ago I began to crave the pleasures of the life of a private man. I determined to go to some sequestered resort where my face was unfamiliar. The possibility of being recognized at Asquith did not occur to me. Fortunately I was. And a singular chance led me to take the name of the man who has committed this crime, and who has the misfortune to resemble me. I suppose that now," he added impressively, "I shall have to tell you who I am."

He paused until these words should have gained their full effect. Then he held up the edition de luxe from which he and Miss Thorn had been reading.

"You may have heard, Mrs. Cooke," said he, addressing himself to our hostess, "you may perhaps have heard of the author of this book."

Mrs. Cooke was a calm woman, and she read the name on the cover.

"Yes," she said, "I have. And you claim to be he?"

"Ask my friend Crocker here," he answered carelessly, no doubt exulting that the scene was going off so dramatically. "I should indeed be in a tight box," he went on, "if there were not friends of mine here to help me out."

They turned to me.

"I am afraid I cannot," I said with what soberness I could.

"What!" says he with a start. "What! you deny me?"

Miss Trevor had her tongue in her cheek. I bowed.

"I am powerless to speak, Mr. Allen," I replied.

During this colloquy my client stood between us, looking from one to the other. I well knew that his way of thinking would be with my testimony, and that the gilt name on the edition de luxe had done little towards convincing him of Mr. Allen's innocence. To his mind there was nothing horrible or incongruous in the idea that a well-known author should be a defaulter. It was perfectly possible. He shoved the glass of Scotch towards the Celebrity, with a smile.

"Take this, old man," he kindly insisted, "and you'll feel better. What's the use of bucking when you're saddled with a thing like that?" And he pointed to the paper. "Besides, they haven't caught you yet, by a damned sight."

The Celebrity waved aside the proffered tumbler.

"This is an infamous charge, and you know it, Crocker," he cried. "If you don't, you ought to, as a lawyer. This isn't any time to have fun with a fellow."

"My dear sir," I said, "I have charged you with nothing whatever."

He turned his back on me in complete disgust. And he came face to face with Miss Trevor.

"Miss Trevor, too, knows something of me," he said.

"You forget, Mr. Allen," she answered sweetly, "you forget that I have given you my promise not to reveal what I know."

The Celebrity chafed, for this was as damaging a statement as could well be uttered against him. But Miss Thorn was his trump card, and she now came forward.

"This is ridiculous, Mr. Crocker, simply ridiculous," said she.

"I agree with you most heartily, Miss Thorn," I replied.

"Nonsense!" exclaimed Miss Thorn, and she drew her lips together, "pure nonsense!"

"Nonsense or not, Marian," Mr. Cooke interposed, "we are wasting valuable time. The police are already on the scent, I'll bet my hat."

"Fenelon!" Mrs. Cooke remonstrated.

"And do you mean to say in soberness, Uncle Fenelon, that you believe the author of The Sybarites to be a defaulter?" said Miss Thorn.

"It is indeed hard to believe Mr. Allen a criminal," Mr.

Trevor broke in for the first time. "I think it only right that he should be allowed to clear himself before he is put to further inconvenience, and perhaps injustice, by any action we may take in the matter."

Mr. Cooke sniffed suspiciously at the word "action."

"What action do you mean?" he demanded.

"Well," replied Mr. Trevor, with some hesitation, "before we take any steps, that is, notify the police."

"Notify the police!" cried my client, his face red with a generous anger. "I have never yet turned a guest over to the police," he said proudly, "and won't, not if I know it. I'm not that kind."

Who shall criticise Mr. Cooke's code of morality?

"Fenelon," said his wife, "you must remember you have never yet entertained a guest of a larcenous character. No embezzlers up to the present. Marian," she continued, turning to Miss Thorn, "you spoke as if you might, be able to throw some light upon this matter. Do you know whether this gentleman is Charles Wrexell Allen, or whether he is the author? In short, do you know who he is?"

The Celebrity lighted a cigarette. Miss Thorn said indignantly, "Upon my word, Aunt Maria, I thought that you, at least, would know better than to credit this silly accusation. He has been a guest at your house, and I am astonished that you should doubt his word."

Mrs. Cooke looked at her niece perplexedly.

"You must remember, Marian," she said gently, "that I know nothing about him, where he came from, or who he is. Nor does any one at Asquith, except perhaps Miss Trevor, by her own confession. And you do not seem inclined to tell what you know, if indeed you know anything."

Upon this Miss Thorn became more indignant still, and Mrs. Cooke went on "Gentlemen, as a rule, do not assume names, especially other people's. They are usually proud of their own. Mr. Allen appears among us, from the clouds, as it were, and in due time we learn from a newspaper that he has committed a defalcation. And, furthermore, the paper contains a portrait and an accurate description which put the thing beyond doubt. I ask you, is it reasonable for him to state coolly after all this that he is another man? That he is a well-known author? It's an absurdity. I was not born yesterday, my dear."

"It is most reasonable under the circumstances," replied Miss Thorn, warmly. "Extraordinary? Of course it's extraordinary. And too long to explain to a prejudiced audience, who can't be expected to comprehend the character of a genius, to understand the yearning of a famous man for a little quiet."

Mrs. Cooke looked grave.

"Marian, you forget yourself," she said.

"Oh, I am tired of it, Aunt Maria," cried Miss Thorn; "if he takes my advice, he will refuse to discuss it farther."

She did not seem to be aware that she had put forth no

argument whatever, save a woman's argument. And I was intensely surprised that her indignation should have got the better of her in this way, having always supposed her clear-headed in the extreme. A few words from her, such as I supposed she would have spoken, had set the Celebrity right with all except Mr. Cooke. To me it was a clear proof that the Celebrity had turned her head, and her mind with it.

The silence was broken by an uncontrollable burst of laughter from Miss Trevor. She was quickly frowned down by her father, who reminded her that this was not a comedy.

"And, Mr. Allen," he said, "if you have anything to say, or any evidence to bring forward, now is the time to do it."

He appeared to forget that I was the district attorney.

The Celebrity had seated himself on the trunk of a tree, and was blowing out the smoke in clouds. He was inclined to take Miss Thorn's advice, for he made a gesture of weariness with his cigarette, in the use of which he was singularly eloquent.

"Tell me, Mr. Trevor," said he, "why I should sit before you as a tribunal? Why I should take the trouble to clear myself of a senseless charge? My respect for you inclines me to the belief that you are laboring under a momentary excitement; for when you reflect that I am a prominent, not to say famous, author, you will realize how absurd it is that I should be an embezzler, and why I decline to lower myself by an explanation."

Mr. Trevor picked up the paper and struck it.

"Do you refuse to say anything in the face of such evidence as that?" he cried.

"It is not a matter for refusal, Mr. Trevor. It is simply that I cannot admit the possibility of having committed the crime."

"Well, sir," said the senator, his black necktie working out of place as his anger got the better of him, "I am to believe, then, because you claim to be the author of a few society novels, that you are infallible? Let me tell you that the President of the United States himself is liable to impeachment, and bound to disprove any charge he may be accused of. What in Halifax do I care for your divine-right-of-authors theory? I'll continue to think you guilty until you are shown to be innocent."

Suddenly the full significance of the Celebrity's tactics struck Mr. Cooke, and he reached out and caught hold of Mr. Trevor's coattails. "Hold on, old man," said he; "Allen isn't going to be ass enough to own up to it. Don't you see we'd all be jugged and fined for assisting a criminal over the border? It's out of consideration for us."

Mr. Trevor looked sternly over his shoulder at Mr. Cooke.

"Do you mean to say, sir, seriously," he asked, "that, for the sake of a misplaced friendship for this man, and a misplaced sense of honor, you are bound to shield a guest, though a criminal? That you intend to assist him to escape from justice? I insist, for my own protection and that of my daughter, as well as for that of the others present that, since he refuses to speak, we must presume him guilty and turn him over."

Mr. Trevor turned to Mrs. Cooke, as if relying on her support.

"Fenelon," said she, "I have never sought to influence your actions when your friends were concerned, and I shall not begin now. All I ask of you is to consider the consequences of your intention."

These words from Mrs. Cooke had much more weight with my client than Mr. Trevor's blustering demands.

"Maria, my dear," he said, with a deferential urbanity, "Mr. Allen is my guest, and a gentleman. When a gentleman gives his word that he is not a criminal, it is sufficient."

The force of this, for some reason, did not overwhelm his wife; and her lip curled a little, half in contempt, half in risibility.

"Pshaw, Fenelon," said she, "what a fraud you are. Why is it you wish to get Mr. Allen over the border, then? "A question which might well have staggered a worthier intellect.

"Why, my dear," answered my client, "I wish to save Mr. Allen the inconvenience, not to say the humiliation, of being brought East in custody and strapped with a pair of handcuffs. Let him take a shooting trip to the great Northwest until the real criminal is caught."

"Well, Fenelon," replied Mrs. Cooke, unable to repress a smile, "one might as well try to argue with a turn-stile or a weather-vane. I wash my hands of it."

But Mr. Trevor, who was both a self-made man and a Western politician, was far from being satisfied. He turned to me with a sweep of the arm he had doubtless learned in the Ohio State Senate.

"Mr. Crocker," he cried, "are you, as attorney of this district, going to aid and abet in the escape of a fugitive from justice?"

"Mr. Trevor," said I, "I will take the course in this matter which seems fit to me, and without advice from any one."

He wheeled on Farrar, repeated the question, and got a like answer.

Brought to bay for a time, he glared savagely around him while groping for further arguments.

But at this point the Four appeared on the scene, much the worse for thickets, and clamoring for luncheon. They had five small fish between them which they wanted Miss Thorn to cook.

CHAPTER XII

The Four received Mr. Cooke's plan for the Celebrity's escape to Canada with enthusiastic acclamation, and as the one thing lacking to make the Bear Island trip a complete success. The Celebrity was hailed with the reverence due to the man who puts up the ring-money in a prize-fight. He was accorded, too, a certain amount of respect as a defaulter, which the Four would have denied him as an author, for I am inclined to the belief that the discovery of his literary profession would have lowered him rather than otherwise in their eyes. My client was naturally anxious to get under way at once for the Canadian border, but was overruled in this by his henchmen, who demanded something to eat. We sat down to an impromptu meal, which was an odd affair indeed. Mrs. Cooke maintained her usual serenity, but said little, while Miss Trevor and I had many a mirthful encounter at the thought of the turn matters had taken.

At the other end of the cloth were Mr. Cooke and the Four, in wonderful spirits and unimpaired appetite, and in their midst sat the Celebrity, likewise in wonderful spirits. His behavior now and again elicited a loud grunt of disapproval from Mr. Trevor, who was plying his knife and fork in a manner emblematic of his state of mind. Mr. Allen was laughing and joking airily with Mr. Cooke and the guests, denying, but not resenting, their accusations with all the sang froid of a hardened criminal. He did not care particularly to go to Canada, he said. Why should he, when he was innocent? But, if Mr. Cooke insisted, he would enjoy seeing that part of the lake and the Canadian side.

Afterwards I perceived Miss Thorn down by the brookside, washing dishes. Her sleeves were drawn back to the elbow, and a dainty white apron covered her blue skirt, while the wind from the lake had disentangled errant wisps of her hair. I stood on the brink above, secure, as I thought, from observation, when she chanced to look up and spied me.

"Mr. Crocker," she called, "would you like to make yourself useful?"

I was decidedly embarrassed. Her manner was as frank and unconstrained as though I had not been shunning her for weeks past.

"If such a thing is possible," I replied.

"Do you know a dish-cloth when you see one?"

I was doubtful. But I procured the cloth from Miss Trevor and returned. There was an air about Miss Thorn that was new to me.

"What an uncompromising man you are, Mr. Crocker," she said to me. "Once a person is unfortunate enough to come under the ban of your disapproval you have nothing whatever to do with them. Now it seems that I have given you offence in some way. Is it not so?"

"You magnify my importance," I said.

"No temporizing, Mr. Crocker," she went on, as though she meant to be obeyed; "sit down there, and let's have it out. I like you too well to quarrel with you."

There was no resisting such a command, and I threw myself on the pebbles at her feet.

"I thought we were going to be great friends," she said. "You and Mr. Farrar were so kind to me on the night of my arrival, and we had such fun watching the dance together."

"I confess I thought so, too. But you expressed opinions then that I shared. You have since changed your mind, for some unaccountable reason."

She paused in her polishing, a shining dish in her hand, and looked down at me with something between a laugh and a frown.

"I suppose you have never regretted speaking hastily," she said.

"Many a time," I returned, warming; "but if I ever thought a judgment measured and distilled, it was your judgment of the Celebrity."

"Does the study of law eliminate humanity?" she asked, with a mock curtsey. "The deliberate sentences are sometimes the unjust ones, and men who are hung by weighed wisdom are often the innocent."

"That is all very well in cases of doubt. But here you have the evidences of wrong-doing directly before you."

Three dishes were taken up, dried, and put down before she answered me. I threw pebbles into the brook, and wished I had held my tongue.

"What evidence?" inquired she. "Well," said I, "I must finish, I suppose. I had a notion you knew of what I inferred. First, let me say that I have no desire to prejudice you against a person whom you admire."

"Impossible."

Something in her tone made me look up.

"Very good, then," I answered. "I, for one, can have no use for a man who devotes himself to a girl long enough to win her affections, and then deserts her with as little compunction as a dog does a rat it has shaken. And that is how your Celebrity treated Miss Trevor."

"But Miss Trevor has recovered, I believe," said Miss Thorn.

I began to feel a deep, but helpless, insecurity.

"Happily, yes," I assented.

"Thanks to an excellent physician."

A smile twitched the corners of her mouth, as though she enjoyed my discomfiture. I remarked for the fiftieth time how strong her face was, with its generous lines and clearly moulded features. And a suspicion entered my soul.

"At any rate," I said, with a laugh, "the Celebrity has got himself into no end of a predicament now. He may go back to New York in custody."

"I thought you incapable of resentment, Mr. Crocker. How mean of you to deny him!"

"It can do no harm," I answered; "a little lesson in the dangers of incognito may be salutary. I wish it were a little lesson in the dangers of something else."

The color mounted to her face as she resumed her occupation.

"I am afraid you are a very wicked man," she said.

Before I could reply there came a scuffling sound from the bank above us, and the snapping of branches and twigs. It was Mr. Cooke. His descent, the personal conduction of which he lost half-way down, was irregular and spasmodic, and a rude concussion at the bottom knocked off a choice bit of profanity which was balanced on the tip of his tongue.

"Tobogganing is a little out of season," said his niece, laughing heartily.

Mr. Cooke brushed himself off, picked up the glasses which he had dropped in his flight and pushed them into my hands. Then he pointed lakeward with bulging eyes.

"Crocker, old man," he said in a loud whisper, "they tell me that is an Asquith cat-boat."

I followed his finger and saw for the first time a sail-boat headed for the island, then about two miles off shore. I raised the glasses.

"Yes," I said, "the Scimitar."

"That's what Farrar said," cried he.

"And what about it?" I asked.

"What about it?" he ejaculated. "Why, it's a detective come for Allen. I knew sure as hell if they got as far as Asquith they wouldn't stop there. And that's the fastest sail-boat he could hire there, isn't it?"

I replied that it was. He seized me by the shoulder and began dragging me up the bank.

"What are you going to do?" I cried, shaking myself loose.

"We've got to get on the Maria and run for it," he panted. "There is no time to be lost."

He had reached the top of the bank and was running towards the group at the tents. And he actually infused me with some of his red-hot enthusiasm, for I hastened after him.

"But you can't begin to get the Maria out before they will be in here," I shouted.

He stopped short, gazed at the approaching boat, and then at me.

"Is that so?"

"Yes, of course," said I, "they will be here in ten minutes."

The Celebrity stood in the midst of the excited Four. His hair was parted precisely, and he had induced a monocle to remain in his eye long enough to examine the Scimitar, his nose at the critical elevation. This unruffled exterior made a deep impression on the Four. Was the Celebrity not undergoing the crucial test of a true sport? He was an example alike to criminals and philosophers.

Mr. Cooke hurried into the group, which divided respectfully for him, and grasped the Celebrity by the hand.

"Something else has got to be done, old man," he said, in a voice which shook with emotion; "they'll be on us before we can get the Maria out."

Farrar, who was nailing a rustic bench near by, straightened up at this, his lip curling with a desire to laugh.

The Celebrity laid his hand on my client's shoulder.

"Cooke," said he, "I'm deeply grateful for all the trouble you wish to take, and for the solicitude you have shown. But let things be. I'll come out of it all right."

"Never," cried Cooke, looking proudly around the Four as some Highland chief might have surveyed a faithful clan. "I'd a damned sight rather go to jail myself."

"A damned sight," echoed the Four in unison.

"I insist, Cooke," said the Celebrity, taking out his eyeglass and tapping Mr. Cooke's purple necktie, "I insist that you drop this business. I repeat my thanks to you and these gentlemen for the friendship they have shown, but say again that I am as innocent of this crime as a baby."

Mr. Cooke paid no attention to this speech. His face became radiant.

"Didn't any of you fellows strike a cave, or a hollow tree, or something of that sort, knocking around this morning?"

One man slapped his knee.

"The very place," he cried. "I fell into it," and he showed a rent in his trousers corroboratively. "It's big enough to hold twenty of Allen, and the detective doesn't live that could find it."

"Hustle him off, quick," said Mr. Cooke.

The mandate was obeyed as literally as though Robin Hood himself had given it. The Celebrity disappeared into the forest, carried rather than urged towards his destined place of confinement.

The commotion had brought Mr. Trevor to the spot. He caught sight of the Celebrity's back between the trees, then he looked at the cat-boat entering the cove, a man in the stern preparing to pull in the tender.

He intercepted Mr. Cooke on his way to the beach.

"What have you done with Mr. Allen?" he asked, in a menacing voice.

"Good God," said Mr. Cooke, whose contempt for Mr. Trevor was now infinite, "you talk as if I were the governor of the state. What the devil could I do with him?"

"I will have no evasion," replied Mr. Trevor, taking an imposing posture in front of him. "You are trying to defeat the ends of justice by assisting a dangerous criminal to escape. I have warned you, sir, and warn you again of the consequences of your meditated crime, and I give you my word I will do all in my power to frustrate it."

Mr. Cooke dug his thumbs into his waistcoat pockets. Here was a complication he had not looked for. The Scimitar lay at anchor with her sail down, and two men were coming ashore in the tender. Mr. Cooke's attitude being that of a man who reconsiders a rash resolve, Mr. Trevor was emboldened to say in a moderated tone:

"You were carried away by your generosity, Mr. Cooke. I was sure when you took time to think you would see it in another light."

Mr. Cooke started off for the place where the boat had grounded. I did not catch his reply, and probably should not have written it here if I had. The senator looked as if he had been sand-bagged.

The two men jumped out of the boat and hauled it up. Mr. Cooke waved an easy salute to one, whom I recognized as the big boatman from Asquith, familiarly known as Captain Jay. He owned the Scimitar and several smaller boats. The captain went through the pantomime of an introduction between Mr.

Cooke and the other, whom my client shook warmly by the hand, and presently all three came towards us.

Mr. Cooke led them to a bar he had improvised by the brook. A pool served the office of refrigerator, and Mr. Cooke had devised an ingenious but complicated arrangement of strings and labels which enabled him to extract any bottle or set of bottles without having to bare his arm and pull out the lot. Farrar and I responded to the call he had given, and went down to assist in the entertainment. My client, with his back to us, was busy manipulating the strings.

"Gentlemen," he said, "let me make you acquainted with Mr. Drew. You all know the captain."

Had I not suspected Mr. Drew's profession, I think I should not have remarked that he gave each of us a keen look as he raised his head. He had reddish-brown hair, and a pair of bushy red whiskers, each of which tapered to a long point. He was broad in the shoulders, and the clothes he wore rather enhanced this breadth. His suit was gray and almost new, the trousers perceptibly bagging at the knee, and he had a felt hat, a necktie of the white and flowery pattern, and square-toed "Congress" boots. In short, he was a decidedly ordinary looking person; you would meet a hundred like him in the streets of Far Harbor and Beaverton. He might have been a prosperous business man in either of those towns, - a comfortable lumber merchant or mine owner. And he had chosen just the get-up I should have picked for detective work in that region. He had a pleasant eye and a very fetching and hearty manner. But his long whiskers troubled me especially. I kept wondering if they were real.

"The captain is sailing Mr. Drew over to Far Harbor," explained Mr. Cooke, "and they have put in here for the night."

Mr. Drew was plainly not an amateur, for he volunteered nothing further than this. The necessary bottles having been produced, Mr. Cooke held up his glass and turned to the stranger.

"Welcome to our party, old man," said he.

Mr. Drew drained his glass and complimented Mr. Cooke on the brand, - a sure key to my client's heart. Whereupon he seated himself between Mr. Drew and the captain and began a discourse on the subject of his own cellar, on which he talked for nearly an hour. His only pauses were for the worthy purpose of filling the detective's or the captain's glass, and these he watched with a hospitable solicitude. The captain had the advantage, three to one, and I made no doubt his employer bitterly regretted not having a boatman whose principles were more strict. At the end of the hour Captain Jay, who by nature was inclined to be taciturn and crabbed, waxed loquacious and even jovial. He sang us the songs he had learned in the winter lumber-camps, which Mr. Cooke never failed to encore to the echo. My client vowed he had not spent a pleasanter afternoon for years. He plied the captain with cigars, and explained to him the mystery of the strings and labels; and the captain experimented until he had broken some of the bottles.

Mr. Cooke was not a person who made any great distinction between the three degrees, acquaintance, friendship, and intimacy. When a stranger pleased him, he went from one to the other with such comparative ease that a hardhearted man, and no other, could have resented his advances. Mr. Drew was anything but a hard-hearted man, and he did not object to my client's familiarity. Mr. Cooke made no secret of his admiration for Mr. Drew, and there were just two things about him that Mr. Cooke admired and wondered at, above all else, - the bushy red whiskers. But it appeared that these were the only things that Mr. Drew was really touchy about. I noticed that the detective, without being impolite, did his best to discourage these remarks; but my client knew no such word as discouragement. He was continually saying: "I think I'll grow some like that, old man," or "Have those cut," and the like, - a kind of humor in which the captain took an incredible delight. And finally, when a certain pitch of good feeling had been arrived at, Mr. Cooke reached out and playfully grabbed hold of the one near him. The detective drew back. "Mr. Cooke," said he, with dignity, "I'll have to ask you to let my whiskers alone."

"Certainly, old man," replied my client, anything but abashed. "You'll pardon me, but they seemed too good to be true. I congratulate you on them."

I was amused as well as alarmed at this piece of boldness, but the incident passed off without any disagreeable results, except, perhaps, a slight nervousness noticeable in the detective; and this soon disappeared. As the sun grew low, the Celebrity's conductors straggled in with fishing-rods and told of an afternoon's sport, and we left the captain peacefully but sonorously slumbering on the bank.

"Crocker," said my client to me, afterwards, "they

didn't feel like the real, home-grown article. But aren't
they damned handsome?"

CHAPTER XIII

After supper, Captain Jay was rowed out and put to bed in his own bunk on the Scimitar. Then we heaped together a huge pile of the driftwood on the beach and raised a blazing beacon, the red light of which I doubt not could be seen from the mainland. The men made prongs from the soft wood, while Miss Thorn produced from the stores some large tins of marshmallows.

The memory of that evening lingers with me yet. The fire colored everything. The waves dashed in ruby foam at our feet, and even the tall, frowning pines at our backs were softened; the sting was gone out of the keen night wind from the north. I found a place beside the gray cape I had seen for the first time the night of the cotillon. I no longer felt any great dislike for Miss Thorn, let it be known. Resentment was easier when the distance between Mohair and Asquith separated us, - impossible on a yachting excursion. But why should I be justifying myself?

Mr. Cooke and the Four, in addition to other accomplishments, possessed excellent voices, and Mr. Drew sang a bass which added much to the melody. One of the Four played a banjo. It is only justice to Mr. Drew to say that he seemed less like a detective than any man I have ever met. He told a good story and was quick at repartee, and after a while the music, by tacit

Winston Churchill

consent, was abandoned for the sake of hearing him talk. He related how he had worked up the lake, point by point, from Beaverton to Asquith, and lightened his narrative with snappy accounts of the different boatmen he had run across and of the different predicaments into which he had fallen. His sketches were so vivid that Mr. Cooke forgot to wink at me after a while and sat spellbound, while I marvelled at the imaginative faculty he displayed. He had us in roars of laughter. His stories were far from incredible, and he looked less like a liar than a detective. He showed, too, an accurate and astonishing knowledge of the lake which could hardly have been acquired in any other way than the long-shore trip he had described. Not once did he hint of a special purpose which had brought him to the island, and it was growing late. The fire died down upon the stones, and the thought of the Celebrity, alone in a dark cave in the middle of the island, began to prey upon me. I was not designed for a practical joker, and I take it that pity is a part of every self-respecting man's composition. In the cool of the night season the ludicrous side of the matter did not appeal to me quite as strongly as in the glare of day. A joke should never be pushed to cruelty. It was in vain that I argued I had no direct hand in the concealing of him; I felt my responsibility quite as heavy upon me. Perhaps bears still remained in these woods. And if a bear should devour the author of The Sybarites, would the world ever forgive me? Could I ever repay the debt to the young women of these United States? To speak truth, I expected every moment to see him appear. Why, in the name of all his works, did he stay there? Nothing worse could befall him than to go to Far Harbor with Drew, where our words concerning his identity would be taken. And what an advertisement this would be for the great author. The Sybarites, now selling by thousands, would increase its sales to ten thousands. Ah, there was the rub. The clue to his remaining in the cave was this very kink in the Celebrity's character. There was nothing Bohemian in that character; it yearned after the eminently respectable. Its very eccentricities were within the limits of good form. The Celebrity shunned the biscuits and beer of the literary clubs, and his books were bound for the boudoir. To have it proclaimed in the sensational journals that the hands of this choice being had been locked for grand larceny was a thought too horrible to entertain. His very manservant would have cried aloud against it. Better a hundred nights in a cave than one such experience!

Miss Trevor's behavior that evening was so unrestful as to lead me to believe that she, too, was going through qualms of sympathy for the victim. As we were breaking up for the evening she pulled my sleeve.

"Don't you think we have carried our joke a little too far, Mr. Crocker?" she whispered uneasily. "I can't bear to think of him in that terrible place."

"It will do him a world of good," I replied, assuming a gayety I did not feel. It is not pleasant to reflect that some day one's own folly might place one in alike situation. And the night was dismally cool and windy, now that the fire had gone out. Miss Trevor began to philosophize.

"Such practical pleasantries as this," she said, "are like infernal machines: they often blow up the people that start them. And they are next to impossible to steer."

"Perhaps it is just as well not to assume we are the

instruments of Providence," I said.

Here we ran into Miss Thorn, who was carrying a lantern.

"I have been searching everywhere for you two mischief-makers," said she. "You ought to be ashamed of yourselves. Heaven only knows how this little experiment will end. Here is Aunt Maria, usually serene, on the verge of hysterics: she says he shouldn't stay in that damp cave another minute. Here is your father, Irene, organizing relief parties and walking the floor of his tent like a madman. And here is Uncle Fenelon insane over the idea of getting the poor, innocent man into Canada. And here is a detective saddled upon us, perhaps for days, and Uncle Fenelon has gotten his boatman drunk. You ought to be ashamed of yourselves," she repeated.

Miss Trevor laughed, in spite of the gravity of these things, and so did I.

"Oh, come, Marian," said she, "it isn't as bad as all that. And you talk as if you hadn't anything to be reproached for. Your own defence of the Celebrity wasn't as strong as it might have been."

By the light of the lantern I saw Miss Thorn cast one meaning look at Miss Trevor.

"What are you going to do about it?" asked Miss Thorn, addressing me. "Think of that unhappy man, without a bed, without blankets, without even a tooth-brush."

"He hasn't been wholly off my mind," I answered

truthfully. "But there isn't anything we can do to-night, with that beastly detective to notice it."

"Then you must go very early to-morrow morning, before the detective gets up."

I couldn't help smiling at the notion of getting up before a detective.

"I am only too willing," I said.

"It must be by four o'clock," Miss Thorn went on energetically, "and we must have a guide we can trust. Arrange it with one of Uncle Fenelon's friends."

"We?" I repeated.

"You certainly don't imagine that I am going to be left behind?" said Miss Thorn.

I made haste to invite for the expedition one of the Four, who was quite willing to go; and we got together all the bodily comforts we could think of and put them in a hamper, the Fraction not forgetting to add a few bottles from Mr. Cooke's immersed bar.

Long after the camp had gone to bed, I lay on the pine-needles above the brook, shielded from the wind by a break in the slope, and thought of the strange happenings of that day. Presently the waning moon climbed reluctantly from the waters, and the stream became mottled, black and white, the trees tall blurs. The lake rose and fell with a mighty rhythm, and the little brook hurried madly over the stones to join it. One thought chased another from my brain.

At such times, when one's consciousness of outer things is dormant, an earthquake might continue for some minutes without one realizing it. I did not observe, though I might have seen from where I lay, the flap of one of the tents drawn back and two figures emerge. They came and stood on the bank above, under the tree which sheltered me. And I experienced a curious phenomenon. I heard, and understood, and remembered the first part of the conversation which passed between them, and did not know it.

"I am sorry to disturb you," said one.

"Not at all," said the other, whose tone, I thought afterwards, betokened surprise, and no great cheerfulness.

"But I have had no other opportunity to speak with you."

"No," said the other, rather uneasily.

Suddenly my senses were alert, and I knew that Mr. Trevor had pulled the detective out of bed. The senator had no doubt anticipated an easier time, and he now began feeling for an opening. More than once he cleared his throat to commence, while Mr. Drew pulled his scant clothing closer about him, his whiskers playing in the breeze.

"In Cincinnati, Mr. Drew," said Mr. Trevor, at length, "I am a known, if not an influential, citizen; and I have served my state for three terms in its Senate."

"I have visited your city, Mr. Trevor," answered Mr. Drew, his teeth chattering audibly, "and I know you by reputation."

"Then, sir," Mr. Trevor continued, with a flourish which appeared absolutely grotesque in his attenuated costume, "it must be clear to you that I cannot give my consent to a flagrant attempt by an unscrupulous person to violate the laws of this country."

"Your feelings are to be respected, sir."

Mr. Trevor cleared his throat again. "Discretion is always to be observed, Mr. Drew. And I, who have been in the public service, know the full value of it."

Mr. Trevor leaned forward, at the same time glancing anxiously up at the tree, for fear, perhaps, that Mr. Cooke might be concealed therein. He said in a stage whisper:

"A criminal is concealed on this island."

Drew started perceptibly.

"Yes," said Mr. Trevor, with a glance of triumph at having produced an impression on a detective, "I thought it my duty to inform you. He has been hidden by the followers of the unscrupulous person I referred to, in a cave, I believe. I repeat, sir, as a man of unimpeachable standing, I considered it my duty to tell you."

"You have my sincere thanks, Mr. Trevor," said Drew, holding out his hand, "and I shall act on the suggestion."

Mr. Trevor clasped the hand of the detective, and they

returned quietly to their respective tents. And in course of time I followed them, wondering how this incident might affect our morning's expedition.

CHAPTER XIV

My first thought on rising was to look for the detective. The touch of the coming day was on the lake, and I made out the two boats dimly, riding on the dead swell and tugging idly at their chains. The detective had been assigned to a tent which was occupied by Mr. Cooke and the Four, and they were sleeping soundly at my entrance. But Drew's blankets were empty. I hurried to the beach, but the Scimitar's boat was still drawn up there near the Maria's tender, proving that he was still on the island.

Outside of the ladies' tent I came upon Miss Thorn, stowing a large basket. I told her that we had taken that precaution the night before.

"What did you put in?" she demanded.

I enumerated the articles as best I could. And when I had finished, she said,

"And I am filling this with the things you have forgotten."

I lost no time in telling her what I had overheard the night before, and that the detective was gone from his tent. She stopped her packing and looked at me in concern.

"He is probably watching us," she said. "Do you think we had better go?"

I thought it could do no harm. "If we are followed," said I, "all we have to do is to turn back."

Miss Trevor came out as I spoke, and our conductor appeared, bending under the hamper. I shouldered some blankets and the basket, and we started. We followed a rough path, evidently cut by a camping party in some past season, but now overgrown. The Fraction marched ahead, and I formed the rear guard. Several times it seemed to me as though someone were pushing after us, and more than once we halted. I put down the basket and went back to reconnoitre. Once I believed I saw a figure flitting in the gray light, but I set it down to my imagination.

Finally we reached a brook, sneaking along beneath the underbrush as though fearing to show itself, and we followed its course. Branches lashed our faces and brambles tore our clothes. And then, as the sunlight was filtering through and turning the brook from blue to crystal, we came upon the Celebrity. He was seated in a little open space on the bank, apparently careless of capture. He did not even rise at our approach. His face showed the effect of a sleepless night, and wore an expression inimical to all mankind. The conductor threw his bundle on the bank and laid his hand on the Celebrity's shoulder.

"Halloa, old man!" said he, cheerily. "You must have had a hard night of it. But we couldn't make you any sooner, because that hawk of an officer had his eye on us."

The Celebrity shook himself free. And in place of the gratitude for which the Fraction had looked, and which he had every reason to expect, he got something different.

"This outrage has gone far enough," said the Celebrity, with a terrible calmness. The Fraction was a man of the world.

"Come, come, old chap!" he said soothingly, "don't cut up. We'll make things a little more homelike here." And he pulled a bottle from the depths of the hamper. "This will brace you up."

He picked up the hamper and disappeared into the place of retention, while the Celebrity threw the bottle into the brush. And just then (may I be forgiven if I am imaginative!) I heard a human laugh come from that direction. In the casting of that bottle the Celebrity had given vent to some of the feelings he had been collecting overnight, and it must have carried about thirty yards. I dived after it like a retriever puppy for a stone; but the bottle was gone! Perhaps I could say more, but it doesn't do to believe in yourself too thoroughly when you get up early. I had nothing to say when I returned.

"You here, Crocker?" said the author, fixing his eye on me. "Deuced kind of you to get up so early and carry a basket so far for me."

"It has been a real pleasure, I assure you," I protested. And it had. There was a silent space while the two young ladies regarded him, softened by his haggard and dishevelled aspect, and perplexed by his attitude. Nothing, I believe, appeals to a woman so much as this very lack of bodily care. And the rogue knew it!

"How long is this little game of yours to continue, - this bull-baiting?" he inquired. "How long am I to be made a butt of for the amusement of a lot of imbeciles?"

Miss Thorn crossed over and seated herself on the ground beside him. "You must be sensible," she said, in a tone that she might have used to a spoiled child. "I know it is difficult after the night you have had. But you have always been willing to listen to reason."

A pang of something went through me when I saw them together. "Reason," said the Celebrity, raising his head. "Reason, yes. But where is the reason in all this? Because a man who happens to be my double commits a crime, is it right that I, whose reputation is without a mark, should be made to suffer? And why have I been made a fool of by two people whom I had every cause to suppose my friends?"

"You will have to ask them," replied Miss Thorn, with a glance at us. "They are mischief-makers, I'll admit; but they are not malicious. See what they have done this morning! And how could they have foreseen that a detective was on his way to the island?"

"Crocker might have known it," said he, melting. "He's so cursed smart!"

"And think," Miss Thorn continued, quick to follow up an advantage, "think what would have happened if they hadn't denied you. This horrid man would have gone off with you to Asquith or somewhere else, with handcuffs on your wrists; for it isn't a detective's place to take evidence, Mr. Crocker says. Perhaps we should all have had to go to Epsom! And I couldn't bear to see you in handcuffs, you know."

"Don't you think we had better leave them alone?" I said to Miss Trevor.

She smiled and shook her head.

"You are blind as a bat, Mr. Crocker," she said.

The Celebrity had weighed Miss Thorn's words and was listening passively now while she talked. There may be talents which she did not possess; I will not pretend to say. But I know there are many professions she might have chosen had she not been a woman. She would have made a name for herself at the bar; as a public speaker she would have excelled. And had I not been so long accustomed to picking holes in arguments I am sure I should not have perceived the fallacies of this she was making for the benefit of the Celebrity. He surely did not. It is strange how a man can turn under such influence from one feeling to another. The Celebrity lost his resentment; apprehension took its place. He became more and more nervous; questioned me from time to time on the law; wished to know whether he would be called upon for testimony at Allen's trial; whether there was any penalty attached to the taking of another man's name; precisely what Drew would do with him if captured; and the tail of his eye was on the thicket as he made this inquiry. It may be surmised that I took an exquisite delight in quenching this new-born thirst for knowledge. And finally we all went into the cave.

Miss Thorn unpacked the things we had brought, while

I surveyed the cavern. It was in the solid rock, some ten feet high and irregular in shape, and perfectly dry. It was a marvel to me how cosy she made it. One of the Maria's lanterns was placed in a niche, and the Celebrity's silver toilet-set laid out on a ledge of the rock, which answered perfectly for a dressing-table. Miss Thorn had not forgotten a small mirror. And as a last office, set a dainty breakfast on a linen napkin on the rock, heating the coffee in a chafing-dish.

"There!" she exclaimed, surveying her labors, "I hope you will be more comfortable."

He had already taken the precaution to brush his hair and pull himself together. His thanks, such as they were, he gave to Miss Thorn. It is true that she had done more than any one else.

"Good-bye, old boy!" said the Fraction. "We'll come back when we get the chance, and don't let that hundred thousand keep you awake."

The Fraction and I covered up the mouth of the cave with brush. He became confidential.

"Lucky dog, Allen!" he said. "They'll never get him away from Cooke. And he can have any girl he wants for the asking. By George! I believe Miss Thorn will elope with him if he ever reaches Canada."

I only mention this as a sample of the Fraction's point of view. I confess the remark annoyed me at the time.

Miss Thorn lingered in the cave for a minute after Miss Trevor came out. Then we retraced our way down the brook, which was dancing now in the sunlight. Miss

Trevor stopped now and then to rest, in reality to laugh. I do not know what the Fraction thought of such heartless conduct. He and I were constantly on the alert for Mr. Drew, but we sighted the camp without having encountered him. It was half-past six, and we had trusted to slip in unnoticed by any one. But, as we emerged from the trees, the bustling scene which greeted our eyes filled us with astonishment. Two of the tents were down, and the third in a collapsed condition, while confusion reigned supreme. And in the midst of it all stood Mr. Cooke, an animated central figure pedestalled on a stump, giving emphatic directions in a voice of authority. He spied us from his elevated position before we had crossed the brook.

"Here they come, Maria," he shouted.

We climbed to the top of the slope, and were there confronted by Mrs. Cooke and Mr. Trevor, with Mr. Cooke close behind them.

"Where the devil is Allen?" my client demanded excitedly of the Fraction.

"Allen?" repeated that gentleman, "why, we made him comfortable and left him, of course. We had sense enough not to bring him here to be pulled."

"But, you damfool," cried Mr. Cooke, slightly forgetting himself, "Drew has escaped."

"Escaped?"

"Yes, escaped," said Mr. Cooke, as though our conductor were personally responsible; "he got away this morning. Before we know it, we'll have the whole police force of Far Harbor out here to jug the lot of us."

The Fraction, being deficient for the moment in language proper to express his appreciation of this new development, simply volunteered to return for the Celebrity, and left in a great hurry.

"Irene," said Mr. Trevor, "can it be possible that you have stolen away for the express purpose of visiting this criminal?"

"If he is a criminal, father, it is no reason that he should starve."

"It is no reason," cried her father, hotly, "why a young girl who has been brought up as you have, should throw every lady-like instinct to the winds. There are men enough in this camp to keep him from starving. I will not have my daughter's name connected with that of a defaulter. Irene, you have set the seal of disgrace upon a name which I have labored for a lifetime to make one of the proudest in the land. And it was my fond hope that I possessed a daughter who - "

During this speech my anger had been steadily rising.. But it was Mrs. Cooke who interrupted him.

"Mr. Trevor," said she, "perhaps you are not aware that while you are insulting your daughter, you are also insulting my niece. It may be well for you to know that Miss Trevor still has my respect as a woman and my admiration as a lady. And, since she has been so misjudged by her father, she has my deepest sympathy. But I wish to beg of you, if you have anything of this nature to say to her, you will take her feelings into consideration as well as ours."

Miss Trevor gave her one expressive look of gratitude. The senator was effectually silenced. He had come, by some inexplicable inference, to believe that Mrs. Cooke, while subservient to the despotic will of her husband, had been miraculously saved from depravity, and had set her face against this last monumental act of outlawry.

VOLUME 4.

CHAPTER XV

I am convinced that Mr. Cooke possessed at least some
of the qualities of a great general. In certain campaigns
of past centuries, and even of this, it has been hero-
worship that impelled the rank and file rather than any
high sympathy with the cause they were striving for.
And so it was with us that morning. Our commander
was everywhere at once, encouraging us to work, and
holding over us in impressive language the awful
alternative of capture. For he had the art, in a high
degree, of inoculating his followers with the spirit
which animated him; and shortly, to my great surprise,
I found myself working as though my life depended on
it. I certainly did not care very much whether the
Celebrity was captured or not, and yet, with the
prospect of getting him over the border, I had not
thought of breakfast. Farrar had a natural inclination
for work of this sort, but even he was infused
somewhat with the contagious haste and enthusiasm
which filled the air; and together we folded the tents
with astonishing despatch and rowed them out to the
Maria, Mr. Cooke having gone to his knees in the
water to shove the boat off.

"What are we doing this for?" said Farrar to me, as we
hoisted the sail.

We both laughed.

"I have just been asking myself that question," I replied.

"You are a nice district attorney, Crocker," he said. "You have made a most proper and equitable decision in giving your consent to Allen's escape. Doesn't your conscience smart?"

"Not unbearably. I'll tell you what, Farrar," said I, "the truth is, that this fellow never embezzled so much as a ten-cent piece. He isn't guilty: he isn't the man."

"Isn't the man?" repeated Farrar.

"No," I answered; "it's a long tale, and no time to tell it now. But he is really, as he claims to be, the author of all those detestable books we have been hearing so much of."

"The deuce he is!" exclaimed Farrar, dropping the stopper he was tying. "Did he write The Sybarites?"

"Yes, sir; he wrote The Sybarites, and all the rest of that trash."

"He's the fellow that maintains a man ought to marry a girl after he has become engaged to her."

"Exactly," I said, smiling at his way of putting it.

"Preaches constancy to all men, but doesn't object to stealing."

I laughed.

"You're badly mixed," I explained. "I told you he never stole anything. He was only ass enough to take the man's name who is the living image of him. And the other man took the bonds."

"Oh, come now," said he, "tell me something improbable while you are about it."

"It's true," I replied, repressing my mirth; "true as the tale of Timothy. I knew him when he was a mere boy. But I don't give you that as a proof, for he might have become all things to all men since. Ask Miss Trevor; or Miss Thorn; she knows the other man, the bicycle man, and has seen them both together."

"Where, in India? Was one standing on the ground looking at his double go to heaven? Or was it at one of those drawing-room shows where a medium holds conversation with your soul, while your body sleeps on the lounge? By George, Crocker, I thought you were a sensible man."

No wonder I got angry. But I might have come at some proper estimation of Farrar's incredulity by that time.

"I suppose you wouldn't take a lady's word," I growled.

"Not for that," he said, busy again with the sail stops; "nor St. Chrysostom's, were he to come here and vouch for it. It is too damned improbable."

"Stranger things than that have happened," I retorted, fuming.

"Not to any of us," he said. Presently he added, chuckling: "He'd better not get into the clutches of that man Drew."

"What do you mean?" I demanded. Farrar was exasperating at times.

"Drew will wind those handcuffs on him like tourniquets," he laughed.

There seemed to be something behind this remark, but before I could inquire into it we were interrupted by Mr. Cooke, who was standing on the beach, swearing and gesticulating for the boat.

"I trust," said Farrar, as we rowed ashore, "that this blind excitement will continue, and that we shall have the extreme pleasure of setting down our friend in Her Majesty's dominions with a yachting-suit and a ham sandwich."

We sat down to a hasty breakfast, in the middle of which the Celebrity arrived. His appearance was unexceptionable, but his heavy jaw was set in a manner which should have warned Mr. Cooke not to trifle with him.

"Sit down, old man, and take a bite before we start for Canada," said my client.

The Celebrity walked up to him.

"Mr. Cooke," he began in a menacing tone, "it is high time this nonsense was ended. I am tired of being made a buffoon of for your party. For your gratification I have spent a sleepless night in those cold, damp woods; and I warn you that practical joking can be carried too far. I will not go to Canada, and I insist that you sail me back to Asquith."

Mr. Cooke winked significantly in our direction and tapped his head.

"I don't wonder you're a little upset, old man," he said, humoringly patting him; "but sit down for a bite of something, and you'll see things differently."

"I've had my breakfast," he said, taking out a cigarette.

Then Mr. Trevor got up.

"He demands, sir, to be delivered over to the authorities," said he, "and you have no right to refuse him. I protest strongly."

"And you can protest all you damn please," retorted my client; "this isn't the Ohio State Senate. Do you know where I would put you, Mr. Trevor? Do you know where you ought to be? In a hencoop, sir, if I had one here. In a hen-coop. What would you do if a man who had gone a little out of his mind asked you for a gun to shoot himself with? Give it him, I suppose. But I put Mr. Allen ashore in Canada, with the funds to get off with, and then my duty's done."

This speech, as Mr. Cooke had no doubt confidently hoped, threw the senator into a frenzy of wrath.

"The day will come, sir," he shouted, shaking his fist at my client, "the day will come when you will rue this bitterly."

"Don't get off any of your oratorical frills on me," replied Mr. Cooke, contemptuously; "you ought to be tied and muzzled."

Mr. Trevor was white with anger.

"I, for one, will not go to Canada," he cried.

"You'll stay here and starve, then," said Mr. Cooke; "damned little I care."

Mr. Trevor turned to Farrar, who was biting his lip.

"Mr. Farrar, I know you to be a rising young man of sound principles, and Mr. Crocker likewise. You are the only ones who can sail. Have you reflected that you are about to ruin your careers?"

"We are prepared to take the chances, I think," said Farrar.

Mr. Cooke looked us over, proudly and gratefully, as much as to say that while he lived we should not lack the necessities of life.

At nine we embarked, the Celebrity and Mr. Trevor for the same reason that the animals took to the ark, - because they had to. There was a spanking breeze in the west-northwest, and a clear sky, a day of days for a sail. Mr. Cooke produced a map, which Farrar and I consulted, and without much trouble we hit upon a quiet place to land on the Canadian side. Our course was north-northwest, and therefore the wind enabled us to hold it without much trouble. Bear Island is situated some eighteen miles from shore, and about equidistant between Asquith and Far Harbor, which latter we had to pass on our way northward.

Although a brisk sea was on, the wind had been steady from that quarter all night, and the motion was uniform. The Maria was an excellent sea-boat. There was no indication, therefore, of the return of that malady which had been so prevalent on the passage to Bear Island. Mr. Cooke had never felt better, and looked every inch a sea-captain in his natty yachting-suit. He had acquired a tan on the island; and, as is eminently proper on a boat, he affected nautical manners and nautical ways. But his vernacular savored so hopelessly of the track and stall that he had been able to acquire no mastery over the art of marine invective. And he possessed not so much as one maritime oath. As soon as we had swung clear of the cove he made for the weather stays, where he assumed a posture not unlike that in the famous picture of Farragut ascending Mobile Bay. His leather case was swung over his shoulder, and with his glasses he swept the lake in search of the Scimitar and other vessels of a like unamiable character.

Although my client could have told you, offhand, jackstraw's last mile in a bicycle sulky, his notion of the Scimitar's speed was as vague as his knowledge of seamanship. And when I informed him that in all probability she had already passed the light on Far Harbor reef, some nine miles this side of the Far Harbor police station, he went into an inordinate state of excitement. Mr. Cooke was, indeed, that day the embodiment of an unselfish if misdirected zeal. He was following the dictates of both heart and conscience in his endeavor to rescue his guest from the law; and true zeal is invariably contagious. What but such could have commanded the unremitting labors of that morning? Farrar himself had done three men's work before breakfast, and it was, in great part, owing to him that we were now leaving the island behind us. He was sailing the Maria that day as she will never be sailed again: her lee gunwale awash, and a wake like a surveyor's line behind her. More than once I called to mind his facetious observation about Mr. Drew, and wondered if he knew more than he had said about the detective.

Once in the open, the Maria showed but small consideration for her passengers, for she went through the seas rather than over them. And Mr. Cooke, manfully keeping his station on the weather bow, likewise went through the seas. No argument could induce him to leave the post he had thus heroically chosen, which was one of honor rather than utility, for the lake was as vacant of sails as the day that Father Marquette (or some one else) first beheld it. Under such circumstances ease must be considered as only a relative term; and the accommodations of the Maria afforded but two comfortable spots, - the cabin, and the lea aft of the cabin bulkhead. This being the case, the somewhat peculiar internal relations of the party decided its grouping.

I know of no worse place than a small yacht, or than a large one for that matter, for uncongenial people. The Four betook themselves to the cabin, which was fortunately large, and made life bearable with a game of cards; while Mrs. Cooke, whose adaptability and sense I had come greatly to, admire, contented herself with a corner and a book. The ungrateful cause of the expedition himself occupied another corner. I caught sight of him through the cabin skylight, and the silver pencil he was holding over his note-book showed unmistakable marks of teeth.

Outside, Mr. Trevor, his face wearing an immutable expression of defiance for the wickedness surrounding him, had placed his daughter for safe-keeping between himself and the only other reliable character on board, - the refrigerator. But Miss Thorn appeared in a blue mackintosh and a pair of heavy yachting-boots, courting rather than avoiding a drenching. Even a mackintosh is becoming to some women. All morning she sat behind Mr. Cooke, on the rise of the cabin, her back against the mast and her hair flying in the wind, and I, for one, was not sorry the Celebrity had given us this excuse for a sail.

CHAPTER XVI

About half-past eleven Mr. Cooke's vigilance was rewarded by a glimpse of the lighthouse on Far Harbor reef, and almost simultaneously he picked up, to the westward, the ragged outline of the house-tops and spires of the town itself. But as we neared the reef the harbor appeared as quiet as a Sunday morning: a few Mackinaws were sailing hither and thither, and the Far Harbor and Beaverton boat was coming out. My client, in view of the peaceful aspect affairs had assumed, presently consented to relinquish his post, and handed the glasses over to me with an injunction to be watchful.

I promised. And Mr. Cooke, feeling his way aft with more discretion than grace, finally descended into the cabin, where he was noisily received. And I was left with Miss Thorn. While my client had been there in front of us, his lively conversation and naive if profane remarks kept us in continual laughter. When with him it was utterly impossible to see any other than the ludicrous side of this madcap adventure, albeit he himself was so keenly in earnest as to its performance. It was with misgiving that I saw him disappear into the hatchway, and my impulse was to follow him. Our spirits, like those in a thermometer, are never stationary: mine were continually being sent up or down. The night before, when I had sat with Miss

Thorn beside the fire, they went up; this morning her anxious solicitude for the Celebrity had sent them down again. She both puzzled and vexed me. I could not desert my post as lookout, and I remained in somewhat awkward suspense as to what she was going to say, gazing at distant objects through the glasses. Her remark, when it came, took me by surprise.

"I am afraid," she said seriously, "that Uncle Fenelon's principles are not all that they should be. His morality is something like his tobacco, which doesn't injure him particularly, but is dangerous to others."

I was more than willing to meet her on the neutral ground of Uncle Fenelon.

"Do you think his principles contagious?" I asked.

"They have not met with the opposition they deserve," she replied. "Uncle Fenelon's ideas of life are not those of other men, - yours, for instance. And his affairs, mental and material, are, happily for him, such that he can generally carry out his notions with small inconvenience. He is no doubt convinced that he is acting generously in attempting to rescue the Celebrity from a term in prison; what he does not realize is that he is acting ungenerously to other guests who have infinitely more at stake."

"But our friend from Ohio has done his best to impress this upon him," I replied, failing to perceive her drift; "and if his words are wasted, surely the thing is hopeless."

"I am not joking," said she. "I was not thinking of Mr. Trevor, but of you. I like you, Mr. Crocker. You may not believe it, but I do." For the life of me I could think of no fitting reply to this declaration. Why was that abominable word "like" ever put into the English language? "Yes, I like you," she continued meditatively, "in the face of the fact that you persist in disliking me."

"Nothing of the kind."

"Oh, I know. You mustn't think me so stupid as all that. It is a mortifying truth that I like you, and that you have no use for me."

I have never known how to take a jest from a woman. I suppose I should have laughed this off. Instead, I made a fool of myself.

"I shall be as frank with you," I said, "and declare that I like you, though I should be much happier if I didn't."

She blushed at this, if I am not mistaken. Perhaps it was unlooked for.

"At any rate," she went on, "I should deem it my duty to warn you of the consequences of this joke of yours. They may not be all that you have anticipated. The consequences for you, I mean, which you do not seem to have taken into account."

"Consequences for me!" I exclaimed.

"I fear that you will think what I am going to say uncalled for, and that I am meddling with something that does not concern me. But it seems to me that you are undervaluing the thing you have worked so hard to attain. They say that you have ability, that you have acquired a practice and a position which at your age give the highest promise for the future. That you are to be counsel for the railroad. In short, that you are the coming man in this section of the state. I have found this out," said she, cutting short my objections, "in spite of the short time I have been here."

"Nonsense!" I said, reddening in my turn.

"Suppose that the Celebrity is captured," she continued, thrusting her hands into the pockets of her mackintosh. "It appears that he is shadowed, and it is not unreasonable to expect that we shall be chased before the day is over. Then we shall be caught red-handed in an attempt to get a criminal over the border. Please wait until I have finished," she said, holding up her hand at an interruption I was about to make. "You and I know he is not a criminal; but he might as well be as far as you are concerned. As district attorney you are doubtless known to the local authorities. If the Celebrity is arrested after a long pursuit, it will avail you nothing to affirm that you knew all along he was the noted writer. You will pardon me if I say that they will not believe you then. He will be taken East for identification. And if I know anything about politics, and especially the state of affairs in local politics with which you are concerned, the incident and the interval following it will be fatal to your chances with the railroad, - to your chances in general. You perceive, Mr. Crocker, how impossible it is to play with fire without being burned."

I did perceive. At the time the amazing thoroughness with which she had gone into the subject of my own unimportant affairs, the astuteness and knowledge of the world she had shown, and the clearness with which she had put the situation, did not strike me. Nothing struck me but the alarming sense of my own stupidity, which was as keen as I have ever felt it. What man in a public position, however humble, has not political enemies? The image of O'Meara was wafted suddenly before me, disagreeably near, and his face wore the smile of victory. All of Mr. Cooke's money could not save me. My spirits sank as the immediate future unfolded itself, and I even read the article in O'Meara's organ, the Northern Lights, which was to be instrumental in divesting me of my public trust and fair fame generally. Yes, if the Celebrity was caught on the other side of Far Harbor, all would be up with John Crocker! But it would never do to let Miss Thorn discover my discomfiture.

"There is something in what you say," I replied, with what bravado I could muster.

"A little, I think," she returned, smiling; "now, what I wish you to do is to make Uncle Fenelon put into Far Harbor. If he refuses, you can go in in spite of him, since you and Mr. Farrar are the only ones who can sail. You have the situation in your own hands."

There was certainly wisdom in this, also. But the die was cast now, and pride alone was sufficient to hold me to the course I had rashly begun upon. Pride! What an awkward thing it is, and more difficult for most of us to swallow than a sponge.

"I thank you for this interest in my welfare, Miss Thorn," I began.

"No fine speeches, please, sir," she cut in, "but do as I advise."

"I fear I cannot."

"Why do you say that? The thing is simplicity itself."

"I should lose my self-respect as a practical joker. And besides," I said maliciously, "I started out to have some fun with the Celebrity, and I want to have it."

"Well," she replied, rather coolly, "of course you can do as you choose."

We were passing within a hundred yards of the lighthouse, set cheerlessly on the bald and sandy tip of the point. An icy silence sat between us, and such a silence is invariably insinuating. This one suggested a horrible thought. What if Miss Thorn had warned me in order to save the Celebrity from humiliation? I thrust it aside, but it returned again and grinned. Had she not practised insincerity before? And any one with half an eye could see that she was in love with the Celebrity; even the Fraction had remarked it. What more natural than, with her cleverness, she had hit upon this means of terminating the author's troubles by working upon my fears?

Human weakness often proves too much for those of us who have the very best intentions. Up to now the refrigerator and Mr. Trevor had kept the strictest and most jealous of vigils over Irene. But at length the senator succumbed to the drowsiness which never failed to attack him at this hour, and he forgot the disrepute of his surroundings in a respectable sleep. Whereupon his daughter joined us on the forecastle.

"I knew that would happen to papa if I only waited long enough," she said. "Oh, he thinks you're dreadful,

Mr. Crocker. He says that nowadays young men haven't any principle. I mustn't be seen talking to you."

"I have been trying to convince Mr. Crocker that his stand in the matter is not only immoral, but suicidal," said Miss Thorn. "Perhaps," she added meaningly, "he will listen to you."

"I don't understand," answered Miss Trevor.

"Miss Thorn has been good enough to point out," I explained, "that the political machine in this section, which has the honor to detest me, will seize upon the pretext of the Celebrity's capture to ruin me. They will take the will for the deed."

"Of course they will do just that," cried Miss Trevor. "How bright of you to think of it, Marian!"

Miss Thorn stood up.

"I leave you to persuade him," said she; "I have no doubt you will be able to do it."

With that she left us, quite suddenly. Abruptly, I thought. And her manner seemed to impress Miss Trevor.

"I wonder what is the matter with Marian," said she, and leaned over the skylight. "Why, she has gone down to talk with the Celebrity."

"Isn't that rather natural?" I asked with asperity.

She turned to me with an amused expression.

"Her conduct seems to worry you vastly, Mr. Crocker. I noticed that you were quite upset this morning in the cave. Why was it?"

"You must have imagined it," I said stiffly.

"I should like to know," she said, with the air of one trying to solve a knotty problem, "I should like to know how many men are as blind as you."

"You are quite beyond me, Miss Trevor," I answered; "may I request you to put that remark in other words?"

"I protest that you are a most unsatisfactory person," she went on, not heeding my annoyance. "Most abnormally modest people are. If I were to stick you with this hat-pin, for instance, you would accept the matter as a positive insult."

"I certainly should," I said, laughing; "and, besides, it would be painful."

"There you are," said she, exultingly; "I knew it. But I flatter myself there are men who would go into an ecstasy of delight if I ran a hat-pin into them. I am merely taking this as an illustration of my point."

"It is a very fine point," said I. "But some people take pleasure in odd things. I can easily conceive of a man gallant enough to suffer the agony for the sake of pleasing a pretty girl."

"I told you so," she pouted; "you have missed it entirely. You are hopelessly blind on that side, and numb. Perhaps you didn't know that you have had a hat-pin sticking in you for some time."

I began feeling myself, nervously.

"For more than a month," she cried, "and to think that you have never felt it." My action was too much for her gravity, and she fell back against the skylight in a fit of merriment, which threatened to wake her father. And I hoped it would.

"It pleases you to speak in parables this morning," I said.

"Mr. Crocker," she began again, when she had regained her speech, "shall I tell you of a great misfortune which might happen to a girl?"

"I should be pleased to hear it," I replied courteously.

"That misfortune, then, would be to fall in love with you."

"Happily that is not within the limits of probability," I answered, beginning to be a little amused. "But why?"

"Lightning often strikes where it is least expected," she replied archly. "Listen. If a young woman were unlucky enough to lose her heart to you, she might do everything but tell you, and you would never know it. I scarcely believe you would know it if she did tell you."

I must have jumped unconsciously.

"Oh, you needn't think I am in love with you."

"Not for a minute," I made haste to say.

She pointed towards the timber-covered hills beyond

the shore.

"Do you see that stream which comes foaming down the notch into the lake in front of us?" she asked. "Let us suppose that you lived in a cabin beside that brook; and that once in a while, when you went out to draw your water, you saw a nugget of - gold washing along with the pebbles on the bed. How many days do you think you would be in coming to the conclusion that there was a pocket of gold somewhere above you, and in starting in search of it?"

"Not long, surely."

"Ah, you are not lacking in perception there. But if I were to tell you that I knew of the existence of such a mine, from various proofs I have had, and that the mine was in the possession of a certain person who was quite willing to share it with you on application, you would not believe me."

"Probably not."

"Well," said Miss Trevor, with a nod of finality, "I was actually about to make such a disclosure. But I see it would be useless."

I confess she aroused my curiosity. No coaxing, however, would induce her to interpret.

"No," she insisted strangely, "if you cannot put two and two together, I fear I cannot help you. And no one I ever heard of has come to any good by meddling."

Miss Trevor folded her hands across her lap. She wore

that air which I am led to believe is common to all women who have something of importance to disclose; or at least what they consider is of importance. There was an element of pity, too, in her expression. For she had given me my chance, and my wits had been found wanting.

Do not let it be surmised that I attach any great value to such banter as she had been indulging in. At the same time, however, I had an uneasy feeling that I had missed something which might have been to my advantage. It was in vain that I whipped my dull senses; but one conclusion was indicated by all this inference, and I don't care even to mention that: it was preposterous.

Then Miss Trevor shifted to a very serious mood. She honestly did her best to persuade me to relinquish our enterprise, to go to Mr. Cooke and confess the whole thing.

"I wish we had washed our hands of this Celebrity from the first," she said, with a sigh. "How dreadful if you lose your position on account of this foolishness!"

"But I shan't," I answered reassuringly; "we are getting near the border now, and no sign of trouble. And besides," I added, "I think Miss Thorn tried to frighten me. And she very nearly succeeded. It was prettily done."

"Of course she tried to frighten you. I wish she had succeeded."

"But her object was transparent."

"Her object!" she exclaimed. "Her object was to save you."

"I think not," I replied; "it was to save the Celebrity."

Miss Trevor rose and grasped one of the sail rings to keep her balance. She looked at me pityingly.

"Do you really believe that?"

"Firmly."

"Then you are hopeless, Mr. Crocker, totally hopeless. I give you up." And she went back to her seat beside the refrigerator.

CHAPTER XVII

"Crocker, old man, Crocker, what the devil does that mean?"

I turned with a start to perceive a bare head thrust above the cabin roof, the scant hair flying, and two large, brown eyes staring into mine full of alarm and reproach. A plump finger was pointing to where the sandy reef lay far astern of us.

The Mackinaws were flecked far and wide over the lake, and a dirty smudge on the blue showed where the Far Harbor and Beaverton boat had gone over the horizon. But there, over the point and dangerously close to the land, hung another smudge, gradually pushing its way like a writhing, black serpent, lakewards. Thus I was rudely jerked back to face the problem with which we had left the island that morning.

I snatched the neglected glasses from the deck and hurried aft to join my client on the overhang, but a pipe was all they revealed above the bleak hillocks of sand. My client turned to me with a face that was white under the tan.

"Crocker," he cried, in a tragic voice, "it's a blessed police boat, or I never picked a winner."

"Nonsense," I said; "other boats smoke beside police boats. The lake is full of tugs."

I was a little nettled at having been scared for a molehill.

"But I know it, sure as hell," he insisted.

"You know nothing about it, and won't for an hour. What's a pipe and a trail of smoke?"

He laid a hand on my shoulder, and I felt it tremble.

"Why do you suppose I came out?" he demanded solemnly.

"You were probably losing," I said.

"I was winning."

"Then you got tired of winning."

But he held up a thumb within a few inches of my face, and with it a ring I had often noticed, a huge opal which he customarily wore on the inside of his hand.

"She's dead," said Mr. Cooke, sadly.

"Dead?" I repeated, perplexed.

"Yes, she's dead as the day I lost the two thousand at Sheepshead. She's never gone back on me yet. And unless I can make some little arrangement with those fellows," he added, tossing his head at the smoke, "you and I will put up to-night in some barn of a jail. I've never been in jail but once," said Mr. Cooke, "and it isn't so damned pleasant, I assure you." I saw that he believed every word of it; in fact, that it was his religion. I might as well have tried to argue the Sultan out of Mohammedanism.

The pipe belonged to a tug, that was certain. Farrar said so after a look over his shoulder, disdaining glasses, and he knew the lake better than many who made their living by it. It was then that I made note of a curious anomaly in the betting character; for thus far Mr. Cooke, like a great many of his friends, was a skeptic. He never ceased to hope until the stake had found its way into the other man's pocket. And it was for hope that he now applied to Farrar. But even Farrar did not attempt to account for the tug's appearance that near the land.

"She's in some detestable hurry to get up this way, that's flat," he said; "where she is, the channel out of the harbor is not forty feet wide."

By this time the rest of the party were gathered behind us on the high side of the boat, in different stages of excitement, scrutinizing the smoke. Mr. Cooke had the glasses glued to his eyes again, his feet braced apart, and every line of his body bespeaking the tension of his mind. I imagined him standing thus, the stump of his cigar tightly clutched between his teeth, following the fortunes of some favorite on the far side of the Belmont track.

We waited without comment while the smoke crept by degrees towards the little white spindle on the tip of the point, now and again catching a gleam of the sun's rays from off the glass of the lantern. And presently, against the white lather of the lake, I thought I caught sight of a black nose pushed out beyond the land. Another moment, and the tug itself was bobbing in the open. Barely had she reached the deep water beyond the sands when her length began to shorten, and the dense cloud of smoke that rose made it plain that she was firing. At the sight I reflected that I had been a fool indeed. A scant flue miles of water lay between us and her, and if they really meant business back there, and they gave every sign of it, we had about an hour and a half to get rid of the Celebrity. The Maria was a good boat, but she had not been built to try conclusions with a Far Harbor tug.

My client, in spite of the ominous condition of his opal, was not slow to make his intentions exceedingly clear. For Mr. Cooke was first and last, and always, a gentleman. After that you might call him anything you pleased. Meditatively he screwed up his glasses and buckled them into the case, and then he descended to the cockpit. It was the Celebrity he singled out of the party.

"Allen," said he, when he stood before him, "I want to impress on you that my word's gold. I've stuck to you thus far, and I'll be damned now if I throw you over, like they did Jonah."

Mr. Cooke spoke with a fine dignity that in itself was impressive, and when he had finished he looked about him until his eye rested on Mr. Trevor, as though opposition were to come from that quarter. And the senator gave every sign of another eruption. But the Celebrity, either from lack of appreciation of my client's loyalty, or because of the nervousness which was beginning to show itself in his demeanor, despite an effort to hide it, returned no answer. He turned on his heel and resumed his seat in the cabin. Mr. Cooke was visibly affected.

"I'd sooner lose my whip hand than go back on him now," he declared.

Then Vesuvius began to rumble.

"Mr. Cooke," said the senator, "may I suggest something which seems pertinent to me, though it does not appear to have occurred to you?"

His tone was the calm one that the heroes used in the Celebrity's novels when they were about to drop on and annihilate wicked men.

"Certainly, sir," my client replied briskly, bringing himself up on his way back to the overhang.

"You have announced your intention of 'standing by' Mr. Allen, as you express it. Have you reflected that there are some others who deserve to be consulted and considered beside Mr. Allen and yourself?"

Mr. Cooke was puzzled at this change of front, and unused, moreover, to that veiled irony of parliamentary expression.

"Talk English, my friend," said he.

"In plain words, sir, Mr. Allen is a criminal who ought to be locked up; he is a menace to society. You, who have a reputation, I am given to understand, for driving four horses, have nothing to lose by a scandal, while I have worked all my life for the little I have achieved, and have a daughter to think about. I will neither stand by Mr. Allen nor by you."

Mr. Cooke was ready with a retort when the true significance of this struck him. Things were a trifle different now. The tables had turned since leaving the island, and the senator held it in his power to ruin our one remaining chance of escape. Strangely enough, he missed the cause of Mr. Cooke's hesitation.

"Look here, old man," said my client, biting off another cigar, "I'm a first-rate fellow when you get to know me, and I'd do the same for you as I'm doing for Allen."

"I daresay, sir, I daresay," said the other, a trifle mollified; "I don't claim that you're not acting as you think right."

"I see it," said Mr. Cooke, with admirable humility; "I see it. I was wrong to haul you into this, Trevor. And the only thing to consider now is, how to get you out of it."

Here he appeared for a moment to be wrapped in deep thought, and checked with his cigar an attempt to interrupt him.

"However you put it, old man," he said at last, "we're all in a pretty bad hole."

"All!" cried Mr. Trevor, indignantly.

"Yes, all," asserted Mr. Cooke, with composure. "There are the police, and here is Allen as good as run down. If they find him when they get abroad, you don't suppose they'll swallow anything you have to say about trying to deliver him over. No, sir, you'll be bagged and fined along with the rest of us. And I'd be damned sorry to see it, if I do say it; and I blame myself freely for it, old man. Now you take my advice and keep your mouth shut, and I'll take care of you. I've got a place for Allen."

During this somewhat remarkable speech Mr. Trevor, as it were, blew hot and cold by turns. Although its delivery was inconsiderate, its logic was undeniable, and the senator sat down again on the locker, and was silent. But I marked that off and on his fingers would open and shut convulsively.

Time alone would disclose what was to happen to us; in the interval there was nothing to do but wait. We had reached the stage where anxiety begins to take the place of excitement, and we shifted restlessly from spot to spot and looked at the tug. She was ploughing along after us, and to such good purpose that presently I began to catch the white of the seas along her bows, and the bright red with which her pipe was tipped. Farrar alone seemed to take but slight interest in her. More than once I glanced at him as he stood under me, but his eye was on the shuddering leach of the sail. Then I leaned over.

"What do you think of it?" I asked.

"I told you this morning Drew would have handcuffs on him before night," he replied, without raising his head.

"Hang your joking, Farrar; I know more than you about it."

"Then what's the use of asking me?"

"Don't you see that I'm ruined if we're caught?" I demanded, a little warmly.

"No, I don't see it," he replied. "You don't suppose I think you fool enough to risk this comedy if the man were guilty, do you? I don't believe all that rubbish about his being the criminal's double, either. That's something the girls got up for your benefit."

I ignored this piece of brutality.

"But I'm ruined anyway."

"How?"

I explained shortly what I thought our friend, O'Meara, would do under the circumstances. An inference sufficed Farrar.

"Why didn't you say something about this before?" he asked gravely. "I would have put into Far Harbor."

"Because I didn't think of it," I confessed.

Farrar pulled down the corners of his mouth with trying not to smile.

"Miss Thorn is a woman of brains," he remarked gently; "I respect her."

I wondered by what mysterious train of reasoning he had arrived at this conclusion. He said nothing for a while, but toyed with the spokes of the wheel, keeping the wind in the sail with undue nicety.

"I can't make them out," he said, all at once.

"Then you believe they're after us?"

"I changed the course a point or two, just to try them."

"And - "

"And they changed theirs."

"Who could have informed?"

"Drew, of course," I said; "who else?"

He laughed.

"Drew doesn't know anything about Allen," said he; "and, besides, he's no more of a detective than I am."

"But Drew was told there was a criminal on the island."

"Who told him?"

I repeated the conversation between Drew and Mr. Trevor which I had overheard. Farrar whistled.

"But you did not speak of that this morning," said he.

"No," I replied, feeling anything but comfortable. At times when he was facetious as he had been this morning I was wont to lose sight of the fact that with Farrar the manner was not the man, and to forget the warmth of his friendship. I was again to be reminded of this.

"Well, Crocker," he said briefly, "I would willingly give up this year's state contract to have known it."

CHAPTER XVIII

It was, accurately as I can remember, half after noon when Mr. Cooke first caught the smoke over the point, for the sun was very high: at two our fate had been decided. I have already tried to describe a part of what took place in that hour and a half, although even now I cannot get it all straight in my mind. Races, when a great deal is at stake, are more or less chaotic: a close four miles in a college eight is a succession of blurs with lucid but irrelevant intervals. The weary months of hard work are forgotten, and you are quite as apt to think of your first velocipede, or of the pie that is awaiting you in the boathouse, as of victory and defeat. And a yacht race, with a pair of rivals on your beam, is very much the same.

As I sat with my feet dangling over the washboard, I reflected, once or twice, that we were engaged in a race. All I had to do was to twist my head in order to make sure of it. I also reflected, I believe, that I was in the position of a man who has bet all he owns, with large odds on losing either way. But on the whole I was occupied with more trivial matters a letter I had forgotten to write about a month's rent, a client whose summer address I had mislaid. The sun was burning my neck behind when a whistle aroused me to the realization that the tug was no longer a toy boat dancing in the distance, but a stern fact but two miles away. There could be no mistake now, for I saw the white steam of the signal against the smoke.

I slid down and went into the cabin. The Celebrity was in the corner by the companionway, with his head on the cushions and a book in his hand. And forward, under the low deck beams beyond the skylight, I beheld the crouching figure of my client. He had stripped off his coat and was busy at some task on the floor.

"They're whistling for us to stop," I said to him.

"How near are they, old man?" he asked, without looking up. The perspiration was streaming down his face, and he held a brace and bit in his hand. Under him was the trap-door which gave access to the ballast below, and through this he had bored a neat hole. The yellow chips were still on his clothes.

"They're not two miles away," I answered. "But what in mystery are you doing there?"

But he only laid a finger beside his nose and bestowed a wink in my direction. Then he took some ashes from his cigar, wetted his finger, and thus ingeniously removed all appearance of newness from the hole he had made, carefully cleaning up the chips and putting them in his pocket. Finally he concealed the brace and bit and opened the trap, disclosing the rough stones of the ballast. I watched him in amazement as he tore a mattress from an adjoining bunk and forced it through the opening, spreading it fore and aft over the stones.

"Now," he said, regaining his feet and surveying the whole with undisguised satisfaction, "he'll be as safe there as in my new family vault."

"But" I began, a light dawning upon me.

"Allen, old man," said Mr. Cooke, "come here."

The Celebrity laid down his book and looked up: my client was putting on his coat.

"Come here, old man," he repeated.

And he actually came. But he stopped when he caught sight of the open trap and of the mattress beneath it.

"How will that suit you?" asked Mr. Cooke, smiling broadly as he wiped his face with an embroidered handkerchief.

The Celebrity looked at the mattress, then at me, and lastly at Mr. Cooke. His face was a study:

"And - And you think I am going to get in there?" he said, his voice shaking.

My client fell back a step.

"Why not?" he demanded. "It's about your size, comfortable, and all the air you want" (here Mr. Cooke stuck his finger through the bit hole). "Damn me, if I were in your fix, I wouldn't stop at a kennel."

"Then you're cursed badly mistaken," said the Celebrity, going back to his corner; "I'm tired of being made an ass of for you and your party."

"An ass!" exclaimed my client, in proper indignation.

"Yes, an ass," said the Celebrity. And he resumed his book.

It would seem that a student of human nature, such as every successful writer should be, might by this time have arrived at some conception of my client's character, simple as it was, and have learned to overlook the slight peculiarity in his mode of expressing himself. But here the Celebrity fell short, if my client's emotions were not pitched in the same key as those of other people, who shall say that his heart was not as large or his sympathies as wide as many another philanthropist?

But Mr. Cooke was an optimist, and as such disposed to look at the best side of his friends and ignore the worst; if, indeed, he perceived their faults at all. It was plain to me, even now, that he did not comprehend the Celebrity's attitude. That his guest should reject the one hope of escape left him was, according to Mr. Cooke, only to be accounted for by a loss of mental balance. Nevertheless, his disappointment was keen. He let down the door and slowly led the way out of the cabin. The whistle sounded shrilly in our ears.

Mr. Cooke sat down and drew a wallet from his pocket. He began to count the bills, and, as if by common consent, the Four followed suit. It was a task which occupied some minutes, and when completed my client produced a morocco note-book and a pencil. He glanced interrogatively at the man nearest him.

"Three hundred and fifty."

Mr. Cooke put it down. It was entirely a matter of course. What else was there to be done? And when he had gone the round of his followers he turned to Farrar and me.

"How much are you fellows equal to?" he asked.

I believe he did it because he felt we should resent being left out: and so we should have. Mr. Cooke's instincts were delicate.

We told him. Then he paused, his pencil in the air, and his eyes doubtfully fixed on the senator. For all this time Mr. Trevor had been fidgeting in his seat; but now he opened his long coat, button by button, and thrust his hand inside the flap. Oh, Falstaff!

"Father, father!" exclaimed Miss Trevor. But her tongue was in her cheek.

I have heard it stated that if a thoroughly righteous man were cast away with ninety and nine ruffians, each of the ruffians would gain one-one-hundredth in virtue, whilst the righteous man would sink to their new level. I am not able to say how much better Mr. Cooke's party was for Mr. Trevor's company, but the senator seemed to realize that something serious had happened to him, for his voice was not altogether steady as he pronounced the amount of his contribution.

"Trevor," cried Mr. Cooke, with great fervor, "I take it all back. You're a true, public-spirited old sport."

But the senator had not yet reached that extreme of degradation where it is pleasurable to be congratulated on wickedness.

My client added up the figures and rubbed his hands. I regret to say that the aggregate would have bought up three small police organizations, body and soul.

"Pull up, Farrar, old man," he shouted.

Farrar released the wheel and threw the Maria into the wind. With the sail cracking and the big boom dodging over our heads, we watched the tug as she drew nearer and nearer, until we could hear the loud beating of her engines. On one side some men were making ready to lower a boat, and then a conspicuous figure in blue stood out by the davits. Then came the faint tinkle of a bell, and the H Sinclair, of Far Harbor, glided up and thrashed the water scarce a biscuit-throw away.

"Hello, there!" the man in uniform called out. It was Captain McCann, chief of the Far Harbor police.

Mr. Cooke waved his cigar politely.

"Is that Mr. Cooke's yacht, the Maria?

"The same," said Mr. Cooke.

"I'm fearing I'll have to come aboard you, Mr. Cooke."

"All right, old man, glad to have you," said my client.

This brought a smile to McCann's face as he got into his boat. We were all standing in the cockpit, save the Celebrity, who was just inside of the cabin door. I had time to note that he was pale, and no more: I must have been pale myself. A few strokes brought the chief to the Maria's stern.

"It's not me that likes to interfere with a gent's pleasure party, but business is business," said he, as he climbed aboard.

My client's hospitality was oriental.

"Make yourself at home, old man," he said, a box of his largest and blackest cigars in his hand. And these he advanced towards McCann before the knot was tied in the painter.

Then a wave of self-reproach swept over me. Was it possible that I, like Mr. Trevor, had been deprived of all the morals I had ever possessed? Could it be that the district attorney was looking calmly on while Mr. Cooke wilfully corrupted the Far Harbor chief-of-police? As agonizing a minute as I ever had in my life was that which it took McCann to survey those cigars. His broad features became broader still, as a huge, red hand was reached out. I saw it close lingeringly over the box, and then Mr. Cooke had struck a match. The chief stepped over the washboard onto the handsome turkey-red cushions on the seats, and thus he came face to face with me.

"Holy fathers!" he exclaimed. "Is it you who are here, Mr. Crocker?" And he pulled off his cap.

"No other, McCann," said I, with what I believe was a most pitiful attempt at braggadocio.

McCann began to puff at his cigar. Clouds of smoke came out of his face and floated down the wind. He was so visibly embarrassed that I gained a little courage.

"And what brings you here?" I demanded.

He scrutinized me in perplexity.

"I think you're guessing, sir."

"Never a guess, McCann. You'll have to explain yourself."

McCann had once had a wholesome respect for me. But it looked now as if the bottom was dropping out of it.

"Sure, Mr. Crocker," he said, "what would you be doing in such company as I'm hunting for? Can it be that ye're helping to lift a criminal over the border?"

"McCann," I asked sternly, "what have you had on the, tug?"

Force of habit proved too much for the man. He went back to the apologetic.

"Never a drop, Mr. Crocker. Upon me soul!"

This reminded Mr. Cooke of something (be it recorded) that he had for once forgotten. He lifted up the top of the refrigerator. The chief's eye followed him. But I was not going to permit this.

"Now, McCann," I commenced again, "if you will state your business here, if you have any, I shall be obliged. You are delaying Mr. Cooke."

The chief was seized with a nervous tremor. I think we were a pair in that, only I managed to keep mine, under. When it came to the point, and any bribing was to be done, I had hit upon a course. Self-respect demanded a dignity on my part. With a painful indecision McCann pulled a paper from his pocket which I saw was a warrant. And he dropped his cigar. Mr. Cooke was quick to give him another.

"Ye come from Bear Island, Mr. Crocker?" he inquired.

I replied in the affirmative.

"I hope it's news I'm telling you," he said soberly; "I'm hoping it's news when I say that I'm here for Mr. Charles Wrexell Allen, - that's the gentleman's name. He's after taking a hundred thousand dollars away from Boston." Then he turned to Mr. Cooke. "The gentleman was aboard your boat, sir, when you left that country place of yours, - what d'ye call it? - Mohair? Thank you, sir." And he wiped the water from his brow. "And they're telling me he was on Bear Island with ye? Sure, sir, and I can't see why a gentleman of your standing would be wanting to get him over the border. But I must do my duty. Begging your pardon, Mr. Crocker," he added, with a bow to me.

"Certainly, McCann," I said.

For a space there was only the bumping and straining of the yacht and the swish of the water against her sides. Then the chief spoke again.

"It will be saving you both trouble and inconvenience, Mr. Crocker, if you give him up, sir."

What did the man mean? Why in the name of the law didn't he make a move? I was conscious that my client was fumbling in his clothes for the wallet; that he had muttered an invitation for the chief to go inside. McCann smoked uneasily.

"I don't want to search the boat, sir."

At these words we all turned with one accord towards the cabin. I felt Farrar gripping my arm tightly from behind.

The Celebrity had disappeared!

It was Mr. Cooke who spoke.

"Search the boat!" he said, something between a laugh and a cry.

"Yes, sir," the chief repeated firmly. "It's sorry I am to do it, with Mr. Crocker here, too."

I have always maintained that nature had endowed my client with rare gifts; and the ease with which he now assumed a part thus unexpectedly thrust upon him, as well as the assurance with which he carried it out, goes far to prove it.

"If there's anything in your linc aboard, chief," he said blandly, "help yourself!"

Some of us laughed. I thought things a little too close to be funny. Since the Celebrity had lost his nerve and betaken himself to the place of concealment Mr. Cooke had prepared for him, the whole composition of the affair was changed. Before, if McCann had arrested the ostensible Mr. Allen, my word, added to fifty dollars from my client, would probably have been sufficient. Should he be found now, no district attorney on the face of the earth could induce the chief to believe that he was any other than the real criminal; nor would any bribe be large enough to compensate McCann for the consequences of losing so important a prisoner. There was nothing now but to carry it off with a high hand. McCann got up.

"Be your lave, Mr. Crocker," he said.

"Never you mind me, McCann," I replied, "but you do what is right."

With that he began his search. It might have been ludicrous if I had had any desire to laugh, for the chief wore the gingerly air of a man looking for a rattlesnake which has to be got somehow. And my client assisted at the inspection with all the graces of a dancing-master. McCann poked into the forward lockers where we kept the stores, - dropping the iron lid within an inch of his toe, - and the clothing-lockers and the sail-lockers. He reached under the bunks, and drew out his hand again quickly, as though he expected to be bitten. And at last he stood by the trap with the hole in it, under which the Celebrity lay prostrate. I could hear my own breathing. But Mr. Cooke had his wits about him still, and at this critical juncture he gave McCann a thump on the back which nearly carried him off his feet.

"They say the mast is hollow, old man," he suggested.

"Be jabers, Mr. Cooke," said McCann, "and I'm beginning to think it is!

"He took off his cap and scratched his head.

"Well, McCann, I hope you're contented," I said.

"Mr. Crocker," said he, "and it's that thankful I am for you that the gent ain't here. But with him cutting high finks up at Mr. Cooke's house with a valet, and him coming on the yacht with yese, and the whole country in that state about him, begorra," said McCann, "and it's domned strange! Maybe it's swimmin' in the water he is!"

The whole party had followed the search, and at this speech of the chief's our nervous tension became suddenly relaxed. Most of us sat down to laugh.

"I'm asking no questions, Mr. Crocker, yell take notice," he remarked, his voice full of reproachful meaning.

"McCann," said I, "you come outside. I want to speak to you."

He followed me out.

"Now," I went on, "you know me pretty well" (he nodded doubtfully), "and if I give you my word that Charles Wrexell Allen is not on this yacht, and never has been, is that sufficient?"

"Is it the truth you're saying, sir?"

I assured him that it was.

"Then where is he, Mr. Crocker?"

"God only knows!" I replied, with fervor. "I don't, McCann."

The chief was satisfied. He went back into the cabin, and Mr. Cooke, in the exuberance of his joy, produced champagne. McCann had heard of my client and of his luxurious country place, and moreover it was the first time he had ever been on a yellow-plush yacht. He tarried. He drank Mr. Cooke's health and looked around him in wonder and awe, and his remarks were worthy of record. These sayings and the thought of the author of The Sybarites stifling below with his mouth to an auger-hole kept us in a continual state of merriment. And at last our visitor rose to go.

As he was stepping over the side, Mr. Cooke laid hold of a brass button and pressed a handful of the black cigars upon him.

"My regards to the detective, old man," said he.

McCann stared.

"My regards to Drew," my client insisted.

"Oh!" said McCann, his face lighting up, "him with the whiskers, what came from Bear Island in a cat-boat. Sure, he wasn't no detective, sir."

"What was he? A police commissioner?"

"Mr. Cooke," said McCann, disdainfully, as he got into his boat, "he wasn't nothing but a prospector doing the lake for one of them summer hotel companies."

CHAPTER XIX

When the biography of the Celebrity is written, and I have no doubt it will be some day, may his biographer kindly draw a veil over that instant in his life when he was tenderly and obsequiously raised by Mr. Cooke from the trap in the floor of the Maria's cabin.

It is sometimes the case that a good fright will heal a feud. And whereas, before the arrival of the H. Sinclair, there had been much dissension and many quarrels concerning the disposal of the quasi Charles Wrexell Allen, when the tug steamed away to the southwards but one opinion remained, - that, like Jonah, he must be got rid of. And no one concurred more heartily in this than the Celebrity himself. He strolled about and smoked apathetically, with the manner of one who was bored beyond description, whilst the discussion was going on between Farrar, Mr. Cooke, and myself as to the best place to land him. When considerately asked by my client whether he had any choice in the matter, he replied, somewhat facetiously, that he could not think of making a suggestion to one who had shown such superlative skill in its previous management.

Mr. Trevor, too, experienced a change of sentiment in Mr. Cooke's favor.

It is not too much to say that the senator's scare had been of such thoroughness that he was willing to agree to almost anything. He had come so near to being relieved of that most precious possession, his respectability, that the reason in Mr. Cooke's course now appealed to him very strongly. Thus he became a tacit assenter in wrong-doing, for circumstances thrust this, once in a while, upon the best of our citizens.

The afternoon wore cool; nay, cold is a better word. The wind brought with it a suggestion of the pine-clad wastes of the northwestern wilderness whence it came, and that sure harbinger of autumn, the blue haze, settled around the hills, and benumbed the rays of the sun lingering over the crests. Farrar and I, as navigators, were glad to get into our overcoats, while the others assembled in the little cabin and lighted the gasoline stove which stood in the corner. Outside we had our pipes for consolation, and the sunset beauty of the lake.

By six we were well over the line, and consulting our chart, w selected a cove behind a headland on our left, which seemed the best we could do for an anchorage, although it was shallow and full of rocks. As we were changing our course to run in, Mr. Cooke appeared, bundled up in his reefer. He was in the best of spirits, and was good enough to concur with our plans.

"Now, sir," asked Farrar, "what do you propose to do with Allen?"

But our client only chuckled.

"Wait and see, old man," he said; "I've got that all fixed."

"Well," Farrar remarked, when he had gone in again, "he has steered it deuced well so far. I think we can trust him."

It was dark when we dropped anchor, a very tired party indeed; and as the Maria could not accommodate us all with sleeping quarters, Mr. Cooke decided that the ladies should have the cabin, since the night was cold. And so it might have been, had not Miss Thorn flatly refused to sleep there. The cabin was stuffy, she said, and so she carried her point. Leaving Farrar and one of Mr. Cooke's friends to take care of the yacht, the rest of us went ashore, built a roaring fire and raised a tent, and proceeded to make ourselves as comfortable as circumstances would allow. The sense of relief over the danger passed produced a kind of lightheartedness amongst us, and the topics broached at supper would not have been inappropriate at a friendly dinner party. As we were separating for the night Miss Thorn said to me:

"I am so happy for your sake, Mr. Crocker, that he was not discovered."

For my sake! Could she really have meant it, after all? I went to sleep thinking of that sentence, beside my client beneath the trees. And it was first in my thoughts when I awoke.

As we dipped our faces in the brook the next morning my client laughed softly to himself between the gasps, and I knew that he had in mind the last consummate touch to his successful enterprise. And the revelation came when the party were assembled at breakfast. Mr. Cooke stood up, and drawing from his pocket a small and mysterious paper parcel he forthwith delivered himself in the tone and manner which had so endeared him to the familiars of the Lake House bar.

"I'm not much for words, as you all know," said he, with becoming modesty, "and I don't set up to be an orator. I am just what you see here, - a damned plain man. And there's only one virtue that I lay any claim to, - no one can say that I ever went back on a friend. I want to thank all of you (looking at the senator) for what you have done for me and Allen. It's not for us to talk about that hundred thousand dollars. - My private opinion is (he seemed to have no scruples about making it public) that Allen is insane. No, old man, don't interrupt me; but you haven't acted just right, and that's a fact. And I won't feel square with myself until I put him where I found him, in safety. I am sorry to say, my friends," he added, with emotion, "that Mr. Allen is about to leave us."

He paused for breath, palpably satisfied with so much of it, and with the effect on his audience.

"Now," continued he, "we start this morning for a place which is only four miles or so from the town of Saville, and I shall then request my esteemed legal adviser, Mr. Crocker, to proceed to the town and buy a ready-made suit of clothes for Mr. Allen, a slouch hat, a cheap necktie, and a stout pair of farmer's boots. And I have here," he said, holding up the package, "I have here the rest of it. My friends, you heard the chief tell me that Drew was doing the lake for a summer hotel syndicate. But if Drew wasn't a detective you can throw me into the lake! He wasn't exactly Pinkerton, and I flatter myself that we were too many for him," said Mr. Cooke, with deserved pride; "and he went away in such a devilish hurry that he forgot his hand-bag with some of his extra things."

Then my client opened the package, and held up on a string before our astonished eyes a wig, a pair of moustaches, and two bushy red whiskers.

And this was Mr. Cooke's scheme! Did it electrify his hearers? Perhaps. Even the senator was so choked with laughter that he was forced to cast loose one of the buttons which held on his turn-down collar, and Farrar retired into the woods. But the gravity of Mr. Cooke's countenance remained serene.

"Old man," he said to the Celebrity, "you'll have to learn the price of potatoes now. Here are Mr. Drew's duplicates; try 'em on."

This the Celebrity politely but firmly refused to do.

"Cooke," said he, "it has never been my lot to visit so kind and considerate a host, or to know a man who pursued his duty with so little thought and care of his own peril. I wish to thank you, and to apologize for any hasty expressions I may have dropped by mistake, and I would it were possible to convince you that I am neither a maniac nor an embezzler. But, if it's just the same to you, I believe I can get along without the disguise you mentioned, and so save Mr. Crocker his pains. In short, if you will set me down at Saville, I am willing to take my chances of reaching the Canadian Pacific from that point without fear of detection."

The Celebrity's speech produced a good impression on all save Mr. Cooke, who appeared a trifle water-logged. He had dealt successfully with Mr. Allen when that gentleman had been in defiant moods, or in moods of ugly sarcasm. But this good-natured, turn-you-down-easy note puzzled my client not a little. Was this cherished scheme a whim or a joke to be lightly cast aside? Mr. Cooke thought not. The determination which distinguished him still sat in his eye as he bustled about giving orders for the breaking of camp. This refractory criminal must be saved from himself, cost what it might, and responsibility again rested heavy on my client's mind as I rowed him out to the Maria.

"Crocker," he said, "if Allen is scooped in spite of us, you have got to go East and make him out an idiot."

He seemed to think that I had a talent for this particular defence. I replied that I would do my best.

"It won't be difficult," he went on; "not near as tough as that case you won for me. You can bring in all the bosh about his claiming to be an author, you know. And I'll stand expenses."

This was downright generous of Mr. Cooke. We have all, no doubt, drawn our line between what is right and what is wrong, but I have often wondered how many of us with the world's indorsement across our backs trespass as little on the other side of the line as he.

After Farrar and the Four got aboard it fell to my lot to row the rest of the party to the yacht. And this was no slight task that morning. The tender was small, holding but two beside the man at the oars, and owing to the rocks and shallow water of which I have spoken, the Maria lay considerably over a quarter of a mile out. Hence each trip occupied some time. Mr. Cooke I had transferred with a load of canvas and the tent poles, and next I returned for Mrs. Cooke and Mr. Trevor, whom I deposited safely. Then I landed again, helped in Miss Trevor and Miss Thorn, leaving the Celebrity for the last, and was pulling for the yacht when a cry from the tender's stern arrested me.

"Mr. Crocker, they are sailing away without us!"

I turned in my seat. The Maria's mainsail was up, and the jib was being hoisted, and her head was rapidly falling off to the wind. Farrar was casting. In the stern, waving a handkerchief, I recognized Mrs. Cooke, and beside her a figure in black, gesticulating frantically, a vision of coat-tails flapping in the breeze. Then the yacht heeled on her course and forged lakewards.

"Row, Mr. Crocker, row! they are leaving us!" cried Miss Trevor, in alarm.

I hastened to reassure her.

"Farrar is probably trying something," I said. "They will be turning presently."

This is just what they did not do. Once out of the inlet, they went about and headed northward, up the coast, and we remained watching them until Mr. Trevor became a mere oscillating black speck against the sail.

"What can it mean?" asked Miss Thorn.

I had not so much as an idea.

"They certainly won't desert us, at any rate," I said. "We had better go ashore again and wait."

The Celebrity was seated on the beach, and he was whittling. Now whittling is an occupation which speaks of a contented frame of mind, and the Maria's departure did not seem to have annoyed or disturbed him.

"Castaways," says he, gayly, "castaways on a foreign shore. Two delightful young ladies, a bright young lawyer, a fugitive from justice, no chaperon, and nothing to eat. And what a situation for a short story, if only an author were permitted to make use of his own experiences!"

"Only you don't know how it will end," Miss Thorn put in.

The Celebrity glanced up at her.

"I have a guess," said he, with a smile.

"Is it true," Miss Trevor asked, "that a story must contain the element of love in order to find favor with the public?"

"That generally recommends it, especially to your sex, Miss Trevor," he replied jocosely.

Miss Trevor appeared interested.

"And tell me," she went on, "isn't it sometimes the case that you start out intent on one ending, and that your artistic sense of what is fitting demands another?"

"Don't be silly, Irene," said Miss Thorn. She was skipping flat pebbles over the water, and doing it capitally, too.

I thought the Celebrity rather resented the question.

"That sometimes happens, of course," said he, carelessly. He produced his inevitable gold cigarette case and held it out to me. "Be sociable for once, and have one," he said.

I accepted.

"Do you know," he continued, lighting me a match, "it beats me why you and Miss Trevor put this thing up on me. You have enjoyed it, naturally, and if you wanted to make me out a donkey you succeeded rather well. I used to think that Crocker was a pretty good friend of mine when I went to his dinners in New York. And I once had every reason to believe," he added, "that Miss Trevor and I were on excellent terms."

Was this audacity or stupidity? Undoubtedly both.

"So we were," answered Miss Trevor, "and I should be very sorry to think, Mr. Allen," she said meaningly, "that our relations had in any way changed."

It was the Celebrity's turn to flush.

"At any rate," he remarked in his most offhand manner, "I am much obliged to you both. On sober reflection I have come to believe that you did the very best thing for my reputation."

CHAPTER XX

He had scarcely uttered these words before the reason for the Maria's abrupt departure became apparent. The anchorage of the yacht had been at a spot whence nearly the whole south of the lake towards Far Harbor was open, whilst a high tongue of land hid that part from us on the shore. As he spoke, there shot before our eyes a steaming tug-boat, and a second look was not needed to assure me that she was the "H. Sinclair, of Far Harbor." They had perceived her from the yacht an hour since, and it was clear that my client, prompt to act as to think, had decided at once to put out and lead her a blind chase, so giving the Celebrity a chance to make good his escape.

The surprise and apprehension created amongst us by her sudden appearance was such that none of us, for a space, spoke or moved. She was about a mile off shore, but it was even whether the chief would decide that his quarry had been left behind in the inlet and turn in, or whether he would push ahead after the yacht. He gave us an abominable five minutes of uncertainty. For when he came opposite the cove he slowed up, apparently weighing his chances. It was fortunate that we were hidden from his glasses by a copse of pines. The Sinclair increased her speed and pushed northward after the Maria. I turned to the Celebrity.

"If you wish to escape, now is your chance," I said.

For contrariness he was more than I have ever had to deal with. Now he crossed his knees and laughed.

"It strikes me you had better escape, Crocker," said he. "You have more to run for."

I looked across at Miss Thorn. She had told him, then, of my predicament. And she did not meet my eye. He began to whittle again, and remarked:

"It is only seventeen miles or so across these hills to Far Harbor, old chap, and you can get a train there for Asquith."

"Just as you choose," said I, shortly.

With that I started off to gain the top of the promontory in order to watch the chase. I knew that this could not last as long as that of the day before. In less than three hours we might expect the Maria and the tug in the cove. And, to be frank, the indisposition of the Celebrity to run troubled me. Had he come to the conclusion that it was just as well to submit to what seemed the inevitable and so enjoy the spice of revenge over me? My thoughts gave zest to my actions, and I was climbing the steep, pine-clad slope with rapidity when I heard Miss Trevor below me calling out to wait for her. At the point of our ascent the ridge of the tongue must have been four hundred feet above the level of the water, and from this place of vantage we could easily make out the Maria in the distance, and note from time to time the gain of the Sinclair.

"It wasn't fair of me, I know, to leave Marian," said Miss Trevor, apologetically, "but I simply couldn't resist the temptation to come up here."

"I hardly think she will bear you much ill will," I answered dryly; "you did the kindest thing possible. Who knows but what they are considering the advisability of an elopement!"

We passed a most enjoyable morning up there, all things taken into account, for the day was too perfect for worries. We even laughed at our hunger, which became keen about noon, as is always the case when one has nothing to eat; so we set out to explore the ridge for blackberries. These were so plentiful that I gathered a hatful for our friends below, and then I lingered for a last look at the boats. I could make out but one. Was it the yacht? No; for there was a trace of smoke over it. And yet I was sure of a mast. I put my hand over my eyes.

"What is it?" asked Miss Trevor, anxiously.

"The tug has the Maria in tow," I said, "and they are coming this way."

We scrambled down, sobered by this discovery and thinking of little else. And breaking through the bushes we came upon Miss Thorn and the Celebrity. To me, preoccupied with the knowledge that the tug would soon be upon us, there seemed nothing strange in the attitude of these two, but Miss Trevor remarked something out of the common at once. How keenly a woman scents a situation.

The Celebrity was standing with his back to Miss

Thorn, at the edge of the water. His chin was in the air, and to a casual observer he looked to be minutely interested in a flock of gulls passing over us. And Miss Thorn? She was enthroned upon a heap of drift-wood, and when I caught sight of her face I forgot the very existence of the police captain. Her lips were parted in a smile.

"You are just in time, Irene," she said calmly; "Mr. Allen has asked me to be his wife."

I stood, with the hatful of berries in my hand, like a stiff wax figure in a museum. The expected had come at last; and how little do we expect the expected when it comes! I was aware that both the young women were looking at me, and that both were quietly laughing. And I must have cut a ridiculous figure indeed, though I have since been informed on good authority that this was not so. Much I cared then what happened. Then came Miss Trevor's reply, and it seemed to shake the very foundations of my wits.

"But, Marian," said she, "you can't have him. He is engaged to me. And if it's quite the same to you, I want him myself. It isn't often, you know, that one has the opportunity to marry a Celebrity."

The Celebrity turned around: an expression of extraordinary intelligence shot across his face, and I knew then that the hole in the well-nigh invulnerable armor of his conceit had been found at last. And Miss Thorn, of all people, had discovered it.

"Engaged to you?" she cried, "I can't believe it. He would be untrue to everything he has written."

"My word should be sufficient," said Miss Trevor, stiffly. (May I be hung if they hadn't acted it all out before.) "If you should wish proofs, however, I have several notes from him which are at your service, and an inscribed photograph. No, Marian," she added, shaking her head, "I really cannot give him up."

Miss Thorn rose and confronted him, and her dignity was inspiring. "Is this so?" she demanded; "is it true that you are engaged to marry Miss Trevor?"

The Bone of Contention was badly troubled. He had undoubtedly known what it was to have two women quarrelling over his hand at the same time, but I am willing to bet that the sensation of having them come together in his presence was new to him.

"I did not think - " he began. "I was not aware that Miss Trevor looked upon the matter in that light, and you know - "

"What disgusting equivocation," Miss Trevor interrupted. "He asked me point blank to marry him, and of course I consented. He has never mentioned to me that he wished to break the engagement, and I wouldn't have broken it."

I felt like a newsboy in a gallery, - I wanted to cheer. And the Celebrity kicked the stones and things.

"Who would have thought," she persisted, "that the author of The Sybarites, the man who chose Desmond for a hero, could play thus idly with the heart of woman? The man who wrote these beautiful lines: 'Inconstancy in a woman, because of the present social conditions, is sometimes pardonable. In a man, nothing is more despicable.' And how poetic a justice it is that he has to marry me, and is thus forced to lead the life of self-denial he has conceived for his hero. Mr. Crocker, will you be my attorney if he should offer any objections?"

The humor of this proved too much for the three of us, and Miss Trevor herself went into peals of laughter. Would that the Celebrity could have seen his own face. I doubt if even he could have described it. But I wished for his sake that the earth might have kindly opened and taken him in.

"Marian," said Miss Trevor, "I am going to be very generous. I relinquish the prize to you, and to you only. And I flatter myself there are not many girls in this world who would do it."

"Thank you, Irene," Miss Thorn replied gravely, "much as I want him, I could not think of depriving you."

Well, there is a limit to all endurance, and the Celebrity had reached his.

"Crocker," he said, "how far is it to the Canadian Pacific?"

I told him.

"I think I had best be starting," said he.

And a moment later he had disappeared into the woods.

We stood gazing in the direction he had taken, until the

sound of his progress had died away. The shock of it all had considerably muddled my brain, and when at last I had adjusted my thoughts to the new conditions, a sensation of relief, of happiness, of joy (call it what you will), came upon me, and I could scarce restrain an impulse to toss my hat in the air. He was gone at last! But that was not the reason. I was safe from O'Meara and calumny. Nor was this all. And I did not dare to look at Miss Thorn. The knowledge that she had planned and carried out with dignity and success such a campaign filled me with awe. That I had misjudged her made me despise myself. Then I became aware that she was speaking to me, and I turned.

"Mr. Crocker, do you think there is any danger that he will lose his way?"

"No, Miss Thorn," I replied; "he has only to get to the top of that ridge and strike the road for Saville, as I told him."

We were silent again until Miss Trevor remarked:

"Well, he deserved every bit of it."

"And more, Irene," said Miss Thorn, laughing; "he deserved to marry you."

"I think he won't come West again for a very long time," said I.

Miss Trevor regarded me wickedly, and I knew what was coming.

"I hope you are convinced, now, Mr. Crocker, that our sex is not as black as you painted it: that Miss Thorn knew what she was about, and that she is not the inconsistent and variable creature you took her to be."

I felt the blood rush to my face, and Miss Thorn, too, became scarlet. She went up to the mischievous Irene and grasping her arms from behind, bent them until she cried for mercy.

"How strong you are, Marian! It is an outrage to hurt me so. I haven't said anything." But she was incorrigible, and when she had twisted free she began again:

"I took it upon myself to speak a few parables to Mr. Crocker the other day. You know, Marian, that he is one of these level-headed old fogies who think women ought to be kept in a menagerie, behind bars, to be inspected on Saturday afternoons. Now, I appeal to you if it wouldn't be disastrous to fall in love with a man of such ideas. And just to let you know what a literal old law-brief he is, when I said he had had a hat-pin sticking in him for several weeks, he nearly jumped overboard, and began to feel himself all over. Did you know that he actually believed you were doing your best to get married to the Celebrity?" (Here she dodged Miss Thorn again.) "Oh, yes, he confided in me. He used to worry himself ill over that. I'll tell you what he said to me only - "

But fortunately at this juncture Miss Trevor was captured again, and Miss Thorn put her hand over her mouth. Heaven only knows what she would have said!

The two boats did not arrive until nearly four o'clock, owing to some trouble to the tug's propeller. Not knowing what excuse my client might have given for leaving some of his party ashore, I thought it best to go out to meet them. Seated on the cabin roof of the Maria I beheld Mr. Cooke and McCann in conversation, each with a black cigar too big for him.

"Hello, Crocker, old man," shouted my client, "did you think I was never coming back? I've had lots of sport out of this hayseed captain" (and he poked that official playfully), "but I didn't get any grub. So we'll have to go to Far Harbor."

I caught the hint. Mr. Cooke had given out that he had started for Saville to restock the larder.

"No," he continued, "Brass Buttons didn't let me get to Saville. You see, when he got back to town last night they told him he had been buncoed out of the biggest thing for years, and they got it into his head that I was child enough to run a ferry for criminals. They told him he wasn't the sleuth he thought he was, so he came back. They'll have the laugh on him now, for sure."

McCann listened with admirable good-nature, gravely pulling at his cigar, and eyeing Mr. Cooke with a friendly air of admiration.

"Mr. Crocker," he said, with melancholy humor, "it's leery I am with the whole shooting-match. Mr. Cooke here is a gentleman, every inch of him, and so be you, Mr. Crocker. But I'm just after taking a look at the hole in the bottom of the boat. 'Ye have yer bunks in queer places, Mr. Cooke,' says I. It's not for me to be doubting a gentleman's word, sir, but I'm thinking me man is over the hills and far away, and that's true for ye."

Mr. Cooke winked expressively.

"McCann, you've been jerked," said he. "Have another bottle!"

The Sinclair towed us to Far Harbor for a consideration, the wind being strong again from the south, and McCann was induced by the affable owner to remain on the yellow-plush yacht. I cornered him before we had gone a great distance.

"McCann," said I, "what made you come back to-day?"

"Faith, Mr. Crocker, I don't care if I am telling you. I always had a liking for you, sir, and bechune you and me it was that divil O'Meara what made all the trouble. I wasn't taking his money, not me; the saints forbid! But glory be to God, if he didn't raise a rumpus whin I come back without Allen! It was sure he was that the gent left that place, - what are ye calling it? - Mohair, in the Maria, and we telegraphs over to Asquith. He swore I'd lose me job if I didn't fetch him to-day. Mr. Crocker, sir, it's the lumber business I'll be startin' next week," said McCann.

"Don't let that worry you, McCann," I answered. "I will see that you don't lose your place, and I give you my word again that Charles Wrexell Allen has never been aboard this yacht, or at Mohair to my knowledge. What is more, I will prove it to-morrow to your satisfaction."

McCann's faith was touching.

"Ye're not to say another word, sir," he said, and he stuck out his big hand, which I grasped warmly.

My affection for McCann still remains a strong one.

After my talk with McCann I was sitting on the forecastle propped against the bitts of the Maria's anchor-chain, and looking at the swirling foam cast up by the tug's propeller. There were many things I wished to turn over in my mind just then, but I had not long been in a state of reverie when I became conscious that Miss Thorn was standing beside me. I got to my feet.

"I have been wondering how long you would remain in that trance, Mr. Crocker," she said. "Is it too much to ask what you were thinking of?"

Now it so chanced that I was thinking of her at that moment. It would never have done to say this, so I stammered. And Miss Thorn was a young woman of tact.

"I should not have put that to so literal a man as you," she declared. "I fear that you are incapable of crossing swords. And then," she added, with a slight hesitation that puzzled me, "I did not come up here to ask you that, - I came to get your opinion."

"My opinion?" I repeated.

"Not your legal opinion," she replied, smiling, "but your opinion as a citizen, as an individual, if you have one. To be frank, I want your opinion of me. Do you happen to have such a thing?"

I had. But I was in no condition to give it.

"Do you think me a very wicked girl?" she asked,

coloring. "You once thought me inconsistent, I believe, but I am not that. Have I done wrong in leading the Celebrity to the point where you saw him this morning?"

"Heaven forbid!" I cried fervently; "but you might have spared me a great deal had you let me into the secret."

"Spared you a great deal," said Miss Thorn. "I - I don't quite understand."

"Well - " I began, and there I stayed. All the words in the dictionary seemed to slip out of my grasp, and I foundered. I realized I had said something which even in my wildest moments I had not dared to think of. My secret was out before I knew I possessed it. Bad enough had I told it to Farrar in an unguarded second. But to her! I was blindly seeking some way of escape when she said softly:

"Did you really care?"

I am man enough, I hope, when there is need to be. And it matters not what I felt then, but the words came back to me.

"Marian," I said, "I cared more than you will ever learn."

But it seems that she had known all the time, almost since that night I had met her at the train. And how? I shall not pretend to answer, that being quite beyond me. I am very sure of one thing, however, which is that I never told a soul, man or woman, or even hinted at it. How was it possible when I didn't know myself?

The light in the west was gone as we were pulled into Far Harbor, and the lamps of the little town twinkled brighter than I had ever seen them before. I think they must have been reflected in our faces, since Miss Trevor, when she came forward to look for us, saw something there and openly congratulated us. And this most embarrassing young woman demanded presently:

"How did it happen, Marian? Did you propose to him?"

I was about to protest indignantly, but Marian laid her hand on my arm.

"Tell it not in Asquith," said she. "Irene, I won't have him teased any more."

We were drawing up to the dock, and for the first time I saw that a crowd was gathered there. The report of this chase had gone abroad. Some began calling out to McCann when we came within distance, among others the editor of the Northern Lights, and beside him I perceived with amusement the generous lines: of the person of Mr. O'Meara himself. I hurried back to give Farrar a hand with the ropes, and it was O'Meara who caught the one I flung ashore and wound it around a pile. The people pressed around, peering at our party on the Maria, and I heard McCann exhorting them to make way. And just then, as he was about to cross the plank, they parted for some one from behind. A breathless messenger halted at the edge of the wharf. He held out a telegram.

McCann seized it and dived into the cabin, followed closely by my client and those of us who could push after. He tore open the envelope, his eye ran over the lines, and then he began to slap his thigh and turn around in a circle, like a man dazed.

"Whiskey!" shouted Mr. Cooke. "Get him a glass of Scotch!"

But McCann held up his hand.

"Holy Saint Patrick!" he said, in a husky voice, "it's upset I am, bottom upwards. Will ye listen to this?"

> "'Drew is your man. Reddish hair and long side whiskers, gray clothes. Pretends to represent summer hotel syndicate. Allen at Asquith unknown and harmless.
>
> "' (Signed.) Everhardt.'"

"Sew me up," said Mr. Cooke; "if that don't beat hell!"

CHAPTER XXI

In this world of lies the good and the bad are so closely intermingled that frequently one is the means of obtaining the other. Therefore, I wish very freely to express my obligations to the Celebrity for any share he may have had in contributing to the greatest happiness of my life.

Marian and I were married the very next month, October, at my client's palatial residence of Mohair. This was at Mr. Cooke's earnest wish: and since Marian was Mrs. Cooke's own niece, and an orphan, there seemed no good reason why my client should not be humored in the matter. As for Marian and me, we did not much care whether we were married at Mohair or the City of Mexico. Mrs. Cooke, I think, had a secret preference for Germantown.

Mr. Cooke quite over-reached himself in that wedding. "The knot was tied," as the papers expressed it, "under a huge bell of yellow roses." The paper also named the figure which the flowers and the collation and other things cost Mr. Cooke. A natural reticence forbids me to repeat it. But, lest my client should think that I undervalue his kindness, I will say that we had the grandest wedding ever seen in that part of the world. McCann was there, and Mr. Cooke saw to it that he had a punchbowl all to himself in which to drink our healths: Judge Short was there, still followed by the conjugal eye: and Senator Trevor, who remained over, in a new long black coat to kiss the bride. Mr. Cooke chartered two cars to carry guests from the East, besides those who came as ordinary citizens. Miss Trevor was of the party, and Farrar, of course, was best man. Would that I had the flow of words possessed by the reporter of the Chicago Sunday newspaper!

But there is one thing I must mention before Mrs. Crocker and I leave for New York, in a shower of rice, on Mr. Cooke's own private car, and that is my client's gift. In addition to the check he gave Marian, he presented us with a huge, 'repousse' silver urn he had had made to order, and he expressed a desire that the design upon it should remind us of him forever and ever. I think it will. Mercury is duly set forth in a gorgeous equipage, driving four horses around the world at a furious pace; and the artist, by special instructions, had docked their tails.

From New York, Mrs. Crocker and I went abroad. And it so chanced, in December, that we were staying a few days at a country-place in Sussex, and the subject of The Sybarites was broached at a dinner-party. The book was then having its sale in England.

"Crocker," said our host, "do you happen to have met the author of that book? He's an American."

I looked across the table at my wife, and we both laughed.

"I happen to know him intimately," I replied.

"Do you, now?" said the Englishman; "what a very

entertaining chap he is, is he not? I had him down in October, and, by Jove, we were laughing the blessed time. He was telling us how he wrote his novels, and he said, 'pon my soul he did, that he had a secretary or something of that sort to whom he told the plot, and the secretary elaborated, you know, and wrote the draft. And he said, 'pon my honor, that sometimes the clark wrote the plot and all, - the whole blessed thing, - and that he never saw the book except to sign his name to it."

"You say he was here in October?" asked Marian, when the laugh had subsided.

"I have the date," answered our host, "for he left me an autograph copy of The Sybarites when he went away." And after dinner he showed us the book, with evident pride. Inscribed on the fly-leaf was the name of the author, October 10th. But a glance sufficed to convince both of us that the Celebrity had never written it.

"John," said Marian to me, a suspicion of the truth crossing her mind, "John, can it be the bicycle man?"

"Yes, it can be," I said; "it is."

"Well," said Marian, "he's been doing a little more for our friend than we did."

Nor was this the last we heard of that meteoric trip through England, which the alleged author of The Sybarites had indulged in. He did not go up to London; not he. It was given out that he was travelling for his health, that he did not wish to be lionized; and there were friends of the author in the metropolis who had never heard of his secretary, and who were at a loss to understand his conduct. They felt slighted. One of these told me that the Celebrity had been to a Lincolnshire estate where he had created a decided sensation by his riding to hounds, something the Celebrity had never been known to do. And before we crossed the Channel, Marian saw another autograph copy of the famous novel.

One day, some months afterwards, we were sitting in our little salon in a Paris hotel when a card was sent up, which Marian took.

"John," she cried, "it's the Celebrity."

It was the Celebrity, in the flesh, faultlessly groomed and clothed, with frock coat, gloves, and stick. He looked the picture of ruddy, manly health and strength, and we saw at once that he bore no ill-will for the past. He congratulated us warmly, and it was my turn to offer him a cigarette. He was nothing loath to reminisce on the subject of his experiences in the wilds of the northern lakes, or even to laugh over them. He asked affectionately after his friend Cooke. Time had softened his feelings, and we learned that he had another girl, who was in Paris just then, and invited us on the spot to dine with her at "Joseph's." Let me say, in passing, that as usual she did credit to the Celebrity's exceptional taste.

"Now," said he, "I have something to tell you two."

He asked for another cigarette, and I laid the box beside him.

"I suppose you reached Saville all right," I said, anticipating.

"Seven at night," said he, "and so hungry that I ate what they call marble cake for supper, and a great many other things out of little side dishes, and nearly died of indigestion afterward. Then I took a train up to the main line. An express came along. 'Why not go West?' I asked myself, and I jumped aboard. It was another whim - you know I am subject to them. When I got to Victoria I wired for money and sailed to Japan; and then I went on to India and through the Suez, taking things easy. I fell in with some people I knew who were going where the spirit moved them, and I went along.

"Algiers, for one place, and whom do you think I saw there, in the lobby of a hotel?"

"Charles Wrexell Allen," cried Marian and I together.

The Celebrity looked surprised. "How did you know?" he demanded.

"Go on with your story," said Marian; "what did he do?"

"What did he do?" said the Celebrity; "why, the blackguard stepped up and shook me by the hand, and asked after my health, and wanted to know whether I were married yet. He was so beastly familiar that I took out my glass, and I got him into a cafe for fear some one would see me with him. 'My dear fellow,' said he, 'you did me the turn of my life. - How can I ever repay you?' 'Hang your impudence,' said I, but I wanted to hear what he had to say. 'Don't lose your temper, old chap,' he laughed; 'you took a few liberties with my name, and there was no good reason why I shouldn't take some with yours. Was there? When I think of it, the thing was most decidedly convenient; it was the hand of Providence.' 'You took liberties with my name,' I cried. With that he coolly called to the waiter to fill our glasses. 'Now,' said he, 'I've got a story for you. Do you remember the cotillon, or whatever it was, that Cooke gave? Well, that was all in the Chicago papers, and the "Miles Standish" agent there saw it, and he knew pretty well that I wasn't West. So he sent me the papers, just for fun. You may imagine my surprise when I read that I had been leading a dance out at Mohair, or some such barbarous place in the northwest. I looked it up on the map (Asquith, I mean), and then I began to think. I wondered who in the devil it might be who had taken my name and occupation, and all that. You see, I had just relieved the company of a little money, and it hit me like a clap of thunder one day that the idiot was you. But I couldn't be sure. And as long as I had to get out very soon anyway, I concluded to go to Mohair and make certain, and then pile things off on you if you happened to be the man.'"

At this point Marian and I were seized with laughter, in which the Celebrity himself joined. Presently he continued:

"'So I went,' said Allen. 'I provided myself with two disguises, as a careful man should, but by the time I reached that outlandish hole, Asquith, the little thing I was mixed up in burst prematurely, and the papers were full of it that morning. The whole place was out with sticks, so to speak, hunting for you. They told me the published description hit you to a dot, all except the scar, and they quarrelled about that. I posed as the promoter of resort syndicates, and I hired the Scimitar and sailed over to Bear Island; and I didn't have a bad time that afternoon, only Cooke insisted on making remarks about my whiskers, and I was in mortal fear lest he might accidentally pull one off. He came cursed near it. By the way, he's the very deuce of a man, isn't he? I knew he took me for a detective, so I played the part. And in the night that ass of a state senator nearly gave me pneumonia by getting me out in the air to tell me they had hid you in a cave. So I sat up all night, and followed the relief party in the morning, and you nearly disfigured me for life when you threw that bottle into the woods. Then I went back to camp, and left so fast that I forgot my extra pair of red whiskers. I had two of each disguise, you know, so I didn't miss them.

"'I guess,' Mr. Allen went on, gleefully, 'that I got off about as cleanly as any criminal ever did, thanks to you. If we'd fixed the thing up between us it couldn't have been any neater, could it? Because I went straight to Far Harbor and got you into a peck of trouble, right away, and then slipped quietly into Canada, and put on the outfit of a travelling salesman. And right here another bright idea struck me. Why not carry the thing farther? I knew that you had advertised a trip to Europe (why, the Lord only knows), so I went East and sailed for England on the Canadian Line. And let me thank you for a little sport I had in a quiet way as the author of The Sybarites. I think I astonished some of your friends, old boy.'"

The Celebrity lighted another cigarette.

"So if it hadn't been for me," he said, "the 'Miles Standish Bicycle Company' wouldn't have gone to the wall. Can they sentence me for assisting Allen to get away, Crocker? If they can, I believe I shall stay over here."

"I think you are safe," said I. "But didn't Allen tell you any more?"

"No. A man he used to know came into the cafe, and Allen got out of the back door. And I never saw him again."

"I believe I can tell you a little more," said Marian.

....

The Celebrity is still writing books of a high moral tone and unapproachable principle, and his popularity is undiminished. I have not heard, however, that he has given way to any more whims.